Jewish Wry

and

Other Slices of Life

Martha Reingold

To the Mintz Girls

Long may they wave!

Contents

Russia-shuna

A Foot in the Door

Preface

I've always been a reader—fiction mostly. People scoff at fiction. They say it's a waste of time, useless fantasy, unimportant in the grand scheme of things. But I read it anyway.

Maybe that's why I've always loved words and word games. I devour the New York Times Sunday Crossword Puzzle. I'd rather play anagrams and banana-grams than eat Baskin Robbins Jamoca Almond Fudge. Charades is a favorite game. The transformation of words into motion is a serious business. And I've always loved art museums and concerts and roaming around parks and hidden gardens. I was destined for a life in the arts. Mostly, people thought I should be a writer.

Now I'm 80 and recently retired. For 60 years I had a career designing and implementing computer software. I was once considered an expert in meta-syntactic languages. Now I have time to consider my options. After suffering from writer's block for over 75 years, I've decided to give writing my best shot. And, I've decided to go public before it's too late.

This book is a collection of pieces I've written in the past year or so. It includes short stories, essays and portions of two memoirs that are currently works in progress.

I want to thank the many friends who have cheered me on. There are a few people who deserve a special "Thank you." My niece, Liz Levine, for her steadfast insistence that I keep on writing, even when I wasn't sure I should. My great friend and sister by choice, Joan McKay, who took me to the International Women's Writing Guild workshop program and really got me going. The Buena Vista Writers' Group in West Hartford who invited me to their meetings and taught me how write in 800 words or less.

And, to my sisters and my sons who listened to me when I probably bored them to death, thanks for your patience and love.

Martha Reingold, 2015

Stories and Essays

Introduction

If you were Jewish and grew up in Brooklyn in the '40s and '50s, you had a unique world view. I grew up in Flatbush, on 17th Street between Avenue I and Avenue J, just a few blocks from Woody Allen's home. We both graduated from Midwood High School, just a year apart. Woody's humor is indigenous to that part of the world. We all delight in black humor, wry quips and neurotic patter. But every now and then, we speak seriously about ourselves and our world. What makes Woody so special, is his talent to get it just right.

Some of my stories are based on people I've met or places I've been. Others are the products of an over-active imagination.

Most of my essays were written from "prompts", words or ideas designed to get the creative juices flowing. Workshops use prompts all the time. Some of my essays were precise responses to the chosen triggers. But sometimes, my mind wandered and I wrote something else. It doesn't really matter. The goal is to get started.

Mrs. Mintz's Blintzes

"*Ai-yi-yi!* I'm fed up with Bella Mintz already!"

Rosie Berg grabbed the Bon Ami can and a piece of steel wool from under the kitchen sink. Weapons in hand she was ready for battle. As she attacked the gas range she cursed her wicked nemesis, under her breath of course. God forbid her Sarah should hear such things.

"That rotten Mrs. Mintz! I ask her how to make blintzes and you know what she answers me? 'That's a family secret!' she says. A family secret? Hoo-ha! Who does she think she is? Fanny Farmer? Even Fanny Farmer shares a recipe!"

Mrs. Berg mumbled a few colorful Yiddish expressions. Sarah shouldn't know from this. Curses were for grownups. Not for her darling girl.

"Already it's May and next week is *Shavuos* and I'll have to make at least two dozen blintzes!" Rosie liked to speak in exclamation points.

Sarah squirmed in her chair. She watched her mother clean up the mess left behind after making a few blintzes. She watched as Mrs. B scrubbed and worked up a sweat trying to scrape a stubborn lump of charred batter off the stove. Rosie moaned and raised her eyes to heaven. She shook some Bon Ami into the big black skillet and scrubbed and scoured furiously to get rid of the burnt butter. The butter washed out, but the skillet turned to rust.

"This rotten skillet has seen better days," she complained. "Come to think of it—so have I."

"*Ai-yi-yi!* Look at the clock! It's time to go to Avenue J and pick up a fresh rye for supper. Sarah. Love of my life. My wondrous girl. Finish eating that blintz already, so I can finish up in here! *Oy vey!* You put sugar on that blintz? Are you *meshuga?* For dessert you use sugar! For lunch you use sour cream!"

Sarah was hacking her way through an over-cooked burnt-edged blintz. Each time she poked it with her fork, blobs of watery cottage cheese belched out from both ends. She closed her eyes, forced a piece between her teeth, swallowed quickly and washed it down with a gulp of Pepsi Cola.

There was a never-ending supply of seltzer and Pepsi Cola in the Berg home. Not milk like the rest of America. Milk and meat at the same time was a sin, and who knew what might happen at any time. No, you didn't drink milk with lunch or supper. Milk was for breakfast or for dessert after a dairy meal. Maybe for coffee (light with two lumps of sugar) or for sneaking into the kitchen at night for another slice of Ebinger's Black Out cake—or—if you were lucky—maybe even some fresh rugelach.

Rosie finished scrubbing.

"Sarah, my angel, do me a favor. Dry the dishes and put them away. Don't mix the dairy with the meat, God forbid! Meantimes, I'll go down and do the laundry. It needs to be on

the line right away. It's a *bisel* cloudy. *Oy gevalt*, I'd better hurry
—it looks like rain!"

Sarah looked out the window where the lilac bushes were
in full bloom swaying in a gentle breeze beneath the sunny
sky.

Rosie tramped down the steps to the dark cellar where a
washing machine stood next to a deep washtub. A basket
overflowing with dirty clothes and bed linen was there, ready
to go. On Monday she did the whites. Tuesday, Sarah ironed
the whites. Wednesday, Rosie did the darks. Thursday, Sarah
ironed the darks. There was no laundry on Friday. Friday was
for getting ready for *Shabbos*. Rosie cooked the food. Sarah
vacuumed and dusted the whole house. Together, they washed
the kitchen baseboards and floor. By supper time, the air was
warm with the smell of food and the house sparkled in the
lamp light. Saturday they rested. Sunday, maybe a little walk,
or a trolley ride to Coney Island. Sarah did her homework and
Rosie collected the laundry for Monday. The week was over.

Back to the cellar. Doing laundry was a tricky business. If
you didn't do it right who would dare hang it out where the
neighbors could see? So Rosie always followed the same
script. The one her mother had taught her. The one she would
teach her Sarah. God willing, her daughter would be trained to
keep up all the Berg traditions like going to *Shul* on *Shabbos*,
keeping a kosher home, cooking chicken soup with giblets and
making blintzes on *Shavuos*.

"*Oy vey*, enough with the blintzes already. I have such a
headache I could *plotz!*"

Here's what she did.

First, she found the clothes with special stains—like beets, or grease or things she couldn't even bear to look at. She turned on the hot water and leaned over the tub where a washboard stood at attention. In her left hand she grabbed the offending article. In her right hand she grabbed a piece of dark laundry soap. She wet them both, leaned over the washboard and scrubbed the poor clothes until all the stains were rubbed away. The dirty water drained away and with it, a bit of her knuckles disappeared as well.

Second, she added water to the washer through a black hose attached to the tub's faucet. She filled it with hot water, added some Rinso soap powder and tossed in the clothes. She diluted some Clorox in the water and mixed it carefully. Not too little —the linen would be grey. Not too much—more than just stains might come out.

She stopped for a minute and smiled. She remembered how she used Ivory Soap Flakes years ago, so that Sarah's little clothes would be soft and fluffy. Like the clouds on the soap box. Sarah was so gorgeous! She could eat her up!

Rosie returned to the task at hand. *So many rules,* she thought. *Ai-yi-yi. I'll never get done!*

She turned on the machine. The agitator swished back and forth and back and forth. The washer shook, it wobbled and it slowly crept farther and farther away from the tub. She scurried alongside waving a wooden paddle looking a lot like Teddy Roosevelt charging up San Juan Hill. She plunged the paddle into the steaming water making sure that each piece was thoroughly washed. When she was satisfied, she turned off the machine, positioned it over a drain in the floor, removed its bottom plug and let the dirty water escape. By this time, the sweat was running down her neck into the space between her massive breasts. Her hair was damp, her feet were steaming and even her teeth were burning up inside her mouth.

The third step. Mrs. B added some clean cold water and turned the machine on for the first rinse. The dancing paddle took an encore. When all the soapsuds disappeared, she drained the water out for the second time. The cold water felt good so she wiped the sweat from her face and let a stream of fresh water run down over her forehead and continue down to cool her burning cheeks.

The fourth step? She filled the machine with some fresh clean cold water again. This time she added bluing from a little bag. Bluing made whites look whiter. *Except when mama adds it to her shampoo.* It usually turned her mother's hair blue or even purple for a day or two. But after that, the hair sparkled.

Rosie turned the machine back on, let it run for a while and drained it for the third and final time.

Now—the *coup de grâce*—she placed a wringer on the top of the washer. It was two heavy rollers with a wooden handle. One by one, she forced a wet piece of laundry between the rollers. Then

> She cranked the handle
> That turned the rollers
> That squeezed the linen
> That gave up its water
> That ran into the drain
> That carried the water away.

When it came out the other end she threw it into a giant wicker basket on the floor. She repeated the drill over and over until all the wash was done and ready to be hung on the line.

Upstairs, Sarah sighed, got up, washed the dirty dishes, dried them and put everything away. She put the blintzes dishes in the dairy closet and the forks and spoons in the dairy drawer. She wet a dishrag and wiped the oilcloth table top and swept the crumbs onto the littered floor. She swept the floor, scooped the crumbs into a dustpan and emptied them into the garbage pail.

She was washing her hands and smiling happily until she glanced out the kitchen window. Rosie was laboring up the cellar steps dragging the damp, full, wicker basket towards the clothes line in the backyard.

Sarah looked down on her mother and Rosie looked up at her special pride and joy. "Sarah honey," she called, "be a good girl. *Oy, oy, oy,* I've got so much to do! Could you go to Avenue J—to the bakery for me?"

Sarah's eyebrows shot north while her grin dove south. *Go shopping for bread? What's with the bread? Every day she needs fresh bread? What is she, crazy?*

"OK," she said.

She got Rosie's pocketbook and waited patiently while her mother rummaged around and pulled out a limp dollar bill. After a pause she pulled out another. *Two dollars?* Sarah knew her day was shot.

"Here's some money, *bubbelah.* Go first to Dubin's and pick up a large loaf bread! Make sure it's a Jewish Rye—with seeds—that goes with pot roast. Not German pumpernickel—that goes with sour cream and herring. And get a half dozen Kaiser rolls—without seeds. They get caught between my teeth. Make sure Mrs. Dubin slices the rye thick. That's better for dunking in the gravy. Thin is for sandwiches.

"I need some grapefruits at the fruit store, and while you're there you can go to the pickle lady and get two or three large sour pickles for us, and one half-sour for your Aunt Ella, she's coming to supper—again.

"And then, if it's not too late, Sarah darling, pop in to Mendelson's and pick up two boxes of Mallomars for noshing. It's May so they might not have any. When it gets hot, they melt. That's all I need! Chocolate! Talk about laundry! My back hurts just thinking about it."

Rosie caught her breath. As she trudged outside to finish the laundry she called over her shoulder, "*Nu*, Sarah, joy of my life, promise for my old age, what are you waiting for? Go, go already!"

As luck would have it, Sarah saw Bella Mintz at the pickle lady's stall. That master chef of all things Jewish was there to buy a schmaltz herring to chop and a pickled herring to eat with a little sour cream on top. Her chopped herring was the envy of every woman in Flatbush.

"Well look who's here? If it isn't Sarah Berg? How are you, *tatele*? *Ai-yi-yi*, you look so good today, I could pinch those rosy cheeks. But no! Not me! I wouldn't dare. You're too big! You'll be getting married any day now, right? Pretty soon we'll make a *shidach*, find you a husband. That won't be so hard with those beautiful cheeks of yours." Forgetting her promise, she gave Sarah's cheek a mighty pinch that brought tears to the poor girl's eyes.

"Oh, I'm so sorry *tatele*, I didn't mean to pinch so hard. Just a little twist for good luck. Right? So tell me, Sarah. How old are you anyway?"

"Sixteen." The conversation was embarrassing but it would have been worse if her mother was with her. Rosie would announce, "She's sixteen. Would you believe it? It's the best age, isn't it?" and Bella Mintz would answer, "I should say so—they're your best friend!" As if Mrs. M would know. She had three sons.

"So how's your mother, Sarah darling? So how's my friend, Rosie Berg?"

"My mother is kind of worried. *Shavuos* is next week and she needs at least two dozen blintzes and she says you make the best blintzes in the whole world but you won't share your recipe with anyone."

Mrs. M raised her eyebrows and lifted her shoulders. "I don't know what you mean. I never heard such a thing."

"Well, she didn't actually say you *won't*—she said you were so busy she wouldn't dare ask you—I think she wouldn't like it if she knew I was asking you—" Her voice sank to a whisper.

There was a long pause and Bella then came up with a plan. "I'll tell you what. You come to my house tomorrow. Me? I'll make a batch of blintzes. I make the blintzes, you watch, you go home and tell your mother how to do it and that's that! Finished. *Fartik.*" Like Pontius Pilate she washed her hands in the air and it was settled.

Thursday morning Sarah arrived at 10:00 a.m. for her blintz-making tutorial. The classroom was Mrs. M's large, sunlit kitchen. It was immaculate. No drippings, no crumbs, no dirty dishes in the sink.

In the center of the kitchen table were three eggs, ½ pound of pot cheese, a small container of cottage cheese, a couple of sticks of butter, a salt shaker and a bottle of Borden's pasteurized milk. There was a tin can full of flour and an empty jelly jar with a picture of Mickey Mouse on one side and Minnie Mouse on the other. There were two bowls, one small and one large, an egg beater, a wooden spoon, a coffee cup and a spotless Pyrex baking dish. A large paper bag had been split open and was lying flat next to the utensils. On the top of the stove was a Wearever Aluminum Heavy Duty Frying Pan with a wooden handle.

It looked like the science lab in Midwood High or maybe a surgeon's sterilized instrument table without the food. Sarah took out her composition book, a sharpened number two pencil and began to make a list.

"Sarah honey, be a good girl. Don't write. Just watch. OK?"

And so the lesson began. Mrs. Mintz did not miss a beat as she worked smoothly and gracefully, all the time explaining what she was doing.

"First! You put the cheese in the little bowl. Add an egg, a little salt—just a pinch with your fingers, you don't measure. Mix it all together 'til it's as smooth as a baby's rear end. Here Sarah, take the spoon—mix it up—a little more—go on—go on—See? One, two three—and you've got your cheese blintzes' fillings all ready. Don't ever use blueberries in your blintzes. The insides come out too runny. A real, honest to God blintz, is stuffed with cheese! Now put the bowl on the side and forget about it, *fershtys*?

"OK. Now. Sarah. Take that big bowl and break in two eggs. Go ahead! Bang hard! They won't bite you! Good. Sarah sweetie, try not to get the eggshells in with the eggs. That's better. Now beat the eggs hard—go, go, beat harder, don't be afraid—they won't bite you! Here, let me show you."

Mrs. M pulled the bowl in front of her imposing bosom and beat the eggs half to death. When she was satisfied, she poured in a little milk, mixed it up, then smiled at a job well done.

"Now watch this part. You have to get it just right to make the *bletlach*."

"*Bletlach?*"

"Of course, the *bletlach*. What did you think? You think you make blintzes without *bletlach?* That's the outside of the blintzes. Just one—that's a *bletel*. Two is already *bletlach*. So if the *bletlach* are no good, the outside of the blintzes are no good and it doesn't matter what you put inside— it's garbage! *Feh!* I wouldn't give it to my worst enemy!

"OK. Let's go. Sarah honey, be a good girl, just watch. No more questions. The *bletlach* have to be just the right thickness. If they're too thin the outside will pop open and the insides will come bursting out just like the lion burst into Daniel's den. If they're too thick, even a chainsaw won't cut through."

Mrs. M got carried away. She raised her hands in the air, shrugged her shoulders, and kissed the "O" she made with her thumb and index finger. It was the combination Jewish-Italian body language used all over Brooklyn.

Sarah was confused. Her mother's *bletlach* were too thick but the insides burst out anyway. But she couldn't worry about that now. She didn't have time to think. It was going so fast she couldn't tell a *bletel* from a pancake.

Mrs. Mintz filled the jelly jar with water and dumped it into the bowl. She put her hand in the tin can, scooped up some flour and threw that in too.

"So *tatele*, to make a good *bletel* you start with the eggs and milk, some water and some flour and you mix it with a wooden spoon to see how it feels—Not too watery, not too much flour—it has to feel right."

She mixed it well, added more water and said "*Geisst Vasser.*" She mixed it well, added some flour and said "*Sheeist May-el.*" It was pancake batter with a Jewish twist. She kept adding water and throwing in flour, all the while saying, "See Sarah, just *Geisst Vasser* and *Sheeist May-el!*" When the bowl was half full she pronounced it ready and handed Sarah the spoon.

"Here give it a spin—a whirl. *Nu?* What are you waiting for? How does it feel? Is good?"

Sarah swished the batter around mindlessly drawing a question mark on top. She had no clue whether it was good or bad or maybe both.

"So, *tatele?* You think it's good? It needs more water? I think so, maybe a *bisel* more. Here, add a drop of water and tell me what you think."

Sarah added a thimbleful of water and mixed it again.

"Perfect! See? You feel it?"

Sarah couldn't see or feel the difference. To please the culinary whizz she nodded her head "yes".

"Now we're going to make all the *bletlach* and after we'll wrap them around some cheese filling and then we'll have blintzes! A miracle! From such simple stuff comes such a delicacy!"

Sarah was supposed to write all this down for her mother. There were three things on the paper: eggs, flour, and a jelly jar. She added "geesst?" and "sheest?" to the list.

"Now pay attention! You want to learn, or you want not to learn. Which is it? Now look. This frying pan is the perfect

size for blintzes. You don't want your *bletlach* to be too small
or too big. You don't want a pan that's too light because if you
want even heat, forget it. It has to have a wooden handle so
you can lift the pan without you should get burned. If you use
an iron skillet, it's no good. It just won't work. Tell that to
your mother. No iron skillet. *Farshteys?*"

The pan was heating up.

"You have to test the heat and the feel of the batter at the
same time. So maybe you lose your first *bletel*. It's a risk you
have to take. You can tell by the first one if the pan is the right
temperature. Also—you can tell if you need to *Geisst* a bit
more *Vasser* or maybe *Sheeist* just a smidgen more *May-el*."

With a firm hand, the Jewish Fanny Farmer took a napkin
in her right hand, attacked the stick of butter until a lump of
butter coated one end of the napkin, picked up the frying pan
with her left hand and smeared the butter over the bottom.
She looked at the pan and nodded her head. The pan was
ready. Next she dipped the coffee cup into the batter, filled it
half way up, poured the batter into the hot buttered pan and
quickly—very, very quickly—she poured the batter back into
the bowl. A thin coating of batter remained in the pan. The
pan went over the flame.

Teacher and pupil watched carefully. The batter bubbled a
little and stuck to the side of the pan for a moment. When the
bubbles popped, the *bletel* became unstuck, the maestro picked
up the pan, flipped it upside down over the brown paper bag
and out came a perfectly symmetrical golden brown crêpe.
"Aha," said Mrs. M, "now *that's* what I call a *bletel!*"

Sarah never moved her eyes. She saw the pattern. Smear
the butter, fill the cup, pour the batter, drain the extra, fry the
bletel, raise the pan, flip it over and then start again. Smear, fill,

pour, drain, fry, raise, flip. Smear, fill, pour, drain, fry, raise, flip. So easy to see. Impossible to copy.

"*Oy vey*, Sarah, wake up! Wake up before you fall off the chair and hit your head on the floor and, God forbid, I have to call an ambulance."

Sarah woke from her trance. By this time there were twelve perfect *bletlach* laying in a semi-circle on the paper bag. The bag was on Mrs. Mintz's left. The bowl of cheese was on her right. In the middle was a clean paper bag and behind the bag was the empty Pyrex dish.

"OK, baby. Here goes!"

With amazing accuracy she lifted a single *bletel*, placed it dark side up on the bag, scooped up a tablespoon of cheese filling and placed it smack in the middle of the delicate circle. Then, in four quick motions she folded the left side in, the right side over, bottom up and top down to form a perfect rectangular blintz which she placed lovingly in its Pyrex home. It was over in a flash and there stood exactly a dozen blintzes in a 4 x 3 pattern and they all fit into the glass dish like a glove.

"Sarah! Wake up!"

"I wasn't sleeping. I was watching."

The glass dish was placed in the icebox for a few minutes to let the blintzes "set". The apprentice wiped the oilcloth while the master cleaned up the kitchen. In ten minutes the kitchen was spotless. There were two full table settings with plates, forks, spoons, napkins and glasses. There was a sugar bowl, a container of Breakstone's Sour Cream and a tall pitcher of iced tea.

"Now. We're not done yet! Not by a long shot! Here's comes the last and final step."

She cut a thick slice of butter and popped it into a large frying pan. When the butter began to bubble but not burn, the Empress of the Kosher Kitchen gently placed four blintzes in the pan. When the bottoms were golden brown she flipped them over and when they were ready she placed them on a paper towel to get off the excess butter. Then she transferred them to the waiting dishes, two blintzes on each plate.

"*Ess, Ess, mein Kind!*" Bella's eyes were glowing. She was beaming. Her bosom was bursting out of her tight, laced-up corset as she watched her young pupil taste the first bite.

Sarah put a spoonful of sugar on her blintzes.

"Take, take," said Mrs. Mintz. "Look at you! You're just skin and bones!"

Sarah sprinkled another spoonful of sugar on her blintzes and added a dollop of sour cream on top of each. She couldn't stop grinning. The look of the golden crust and the smell of the warm cheese in each blintz transported her to another world. Carefully she sunk her fork into a blintz and lifted a piece of perfection to her lips.

The two sat together for quite a while—the young girl drunk on the surfeit of good food—the old woman drunk with the joy of cooking up such a lovely treat. She was proud of her skill. Making blintzes was a dying art but she wouldn't let that happen. She would never be forgotten because, without a doubt, she was the Blintzes Queen of Brooklyn!

When Sarah was leaving, Bella gave her a big hug. With a tear in her eye she said, "Don't forget to tell your mama that it's all in the flip of the wrist. Oh. And be sure to tell her just to '*Geisst Vasser* and *Sheeist May-el* 'til it's just right. And Sarah honey, be a good girl and come see me again? I wish I had a daughter just like you. Maybe, if God's willing, he'll make a miracle. If the Bible Sarah could do it, why not me? So come back and maybe next time I'll show you how to chop some liver!"

Rosie was on the stoop waiting for Sarah to come home.

"What took you so long? I was so worried I could have dropped dead! I thought you maybe got hit by a truck—or maybe you were lying dead in some alley. *Nu?* So? You got the recipe?"

Sarah looked at her pad.

"You don't really need a recipe, mom. It's all about using the right frying pan and then you pop each *bletel* out with a twist and a flip."

"What? That's all she told you?"

"Oh! I forgot. She told me all you have to do is send the geese to Vassar and put the cheese in the mail."

Sarah thought about that for a minute. Then she let out a yelp and ran into the backyard to bring in the laundry. It looked like it might rain.

Grant's on Farmington

It was 4:30 in the afternoon and Helen sat sipping sherry at her usual table outside Grant's on Farmington Avenue. "Taking a nip of the old cooking sherry?" her daughters used to tease her. But they were off at college now. Helen sighed happily. She took another sip and said, "If I had a Pall Mall, the day would be perfect."

Nobody turned around when Helen talked to herself. A few of them were talking into mikes clipped onto their heads like aliens with antennae popping out of their skulls. Most of them were texting and their thumbs were getting stronger and stronger at the same time as their pinky fingers were turning into vestigial appendages.

Helen talked to herself a lot lately, what with Jan and Sylvie both away. Thinking about her daughters she frowned, gulped down her sherry and ordered another. Her usual waiter raised his eyebrows, shrugged his shoulders and walked inside. This lady *never* ordered two drinks.

She stared at the couple at the next table. He was reading the latest stock quotes on his blue iPad. She was calculating the cost of a new BMW on her rose colored iPad.

Helen tried to concentrate on something—anything—just not on her girls. Still, images kept flashing before her eyes.

Cool, aloof Jan up North. She was skiing on some mushy slope in Maine ready to break a bone or two. Helen would have to go up to that god-forsaken place where weather beaten old farmers looked at you from under sprouting eyebrows and said "Ya' can't get them from he-yah."

Sexy, in-your-face Sylvie, as far South as she could go. She was strutting down the halls of the co-ed dorm wearing thongs under her short-short-short see-through pants. She pictured Sylvie prancing around on a nudie beach where Helen would have to go, lay her whimpering daughter face-down on a stretcher and fly her home. There she would have to tend Sylvie's second degree burns—all over her body—in places too embarrassing to mention.

Jan was a senior with a 3.8 GPA. If she survived living in Maine, she would go on to get her MBA, land a Wall Street job, earn a high six-figure salary, meet a smart young investment broker and, with their combined seven-figure salaries, they would buy a $3,000,000 glass apartment on Central Park South with a 360° view. They would never have to go outside to see the park or the Hudson River or SoHo or NoHo where majestic buildings rose like the Phoenix from the ashes of abandoned warehouses.

Sylvie was a freshman—again—and would be lucky if she made it to the end of the year without getting knocked up. She would move to some commune or ashram where she would wear worn out Birkenstocks, her dirty toenails sticking out as she brazenly nursed the twins—one on each side—all the while eating kale and Brussel sprouts with a side dish of cous-cous and lemon.

Helen didn't want to think about it. So she sat at Grant's on Farmington Avenue and people-watched instead.

There were the 30-something yuppies on their way home from work heading for the Elbow Room to drown their chagrin in alcohol. They were not prepared for a world that expected them to work without the admiration and praise they deserved. They drank and laughed and talked about the old farts who couldn't tell their asses from their elbows.

There were the 40-something mothers pushing strollers at breakneck speeds, rushing home to set their pre-cooked over-priced Whole Foods dinner on the table.

There were the baby boomers coming out of the Toy Chest where they had just bought toys for the grandchildren to destroy. This group waited patiently for the "Walk" light so they could go to CVS and pick up Lipitor for their cholesterol and baby aspirin to keep their blood from clotting. Then they went on to an early bird special for a cheeseburger with a side order of fries.

Helen sighed. It was the same thing day after day. Not at all like it was in New York. There she would go to Grant's on Broadway and people-watch a much more interesting crowd.

There were the men dressed in full-length mink coats. There were up-tight women carrying Bergdorf shopping bags as they clicked along, perfectly balanced on 4-inch high stiletto heels. In another time they could have passed for hookers. Now, with their perfect skin, aquiline noses, tiny waists and boyish hips they could very well be high-priced hookers masquerading as Ralph Lauren anorexic, breast-less, teen-age models.

Every day when the weather was good, the Purple Lady appeared completely decked out in that regal hue. In the summer she stepped out of a bus wearing purple hats with brims so wide she needed two seats. In the winter she wore purple leather snow boots adorned with lavender rabbit fur.

Helen remembered with delight the day she was eating at the West Side Café on Columbus sitting in the sun, chatting with a friend. They were drinking Mango Tequilas waiting for their salads to arrive. A shadow fell over the table as a man in disreputable attire leaned over the railing and took two multi-grain rolls from their basket. Then he sauntered to the next table and lifted a turkey and cheese panini in pesto sauce. At the third table he swiped a health salad with beets and feta cheese, plate and all. He put his loot in a "Save the Earth" reusable shopping bag, nonchalantly turned the corner and headed east. On her way home Helen passed him picnicking in Central Park, dining on the bounty he had pinched and washing it all down with a beer he had appropriated from a trendy take-out food store.

At 5:30 Helen's happy hour was up. Oh, how she wished she were back in New York sipping sherry and nibbling pretzels as she examined the assorted nuts passing by. But she knew that wouldn't be enough. In New York, she could go to museums and movies and the opera and the ballet. But even that wouldn't be enough.

What Helen really wanted was for Jan and Sylvie to come home and the three of them would live together. They would argue and fight and scream at each other. Jan would give them the holier-than-thou act. Sylvie would flounce out the door and come back sloshed. Helen would cry and moan and drown her frustration in Rocky Road ice cream with hot fudge and sprinkles.

But hey! Isn't that what are families for?

The Umpteenth Draft

I love John McFee. He's the best, the brightest, the most brilliant—he's the cat's pajamas! What can I say? Old and wrinkled as I am, John McFee can put his shoes under my bed any time he wants.

John McFee wrote an essay for me and had it published in the New Yorker. It is called "The 4th Draft". In it he says that to be a good writer you have to be willing to re-write what you have written at least four times. So, that makes me the greatest writer on Earth. I can't begin to tell you how many times I've rewritten and rewritten and rewritten a piece—every piece.

If I put a notch on my gun for every time I've rewritten something, I would need more guns than Charlton Heston. If I put a tick mark on the wall and crossed off every fifth one, I would have, hands down, more tick marks than that man in "The Kiss of the Spider Woman".

First I write something and next I bore people to death until they desperately try to escape. When I walk into a room, they fade away like the "Foggy, foggy dew".

I call my sister and ask *"Can I read it to you?"* and before she can whisper *"Again?"* I'm up and running.

When I see my shrink I tell him that the thing I gave him to read last time needs some more work and then I bring back a corrected copy, but still unfinished manuscript, two weeks later.

The dentist asks me, "So what are you doing now that you're retired?" And I go home and write a poem about him and email it to him and when he doesn't acknowledge it, I figure either I insulted him or it stinks. Either way, it must be rewritten.

Each time I change something, I try it out on my cat. Tootsie is my barometer. If she runs away, I throw it away. If she yawns, I run to my overworked laptop and start again. If she doesn't move, I wait until the next day to begin the next draft.

Last summer I decided to hone my skills. I took eight hours of a metaphor workshop and honestly believed I learned a lot. Unfortunately, I only reduced the number of rewrites by ten percent.

If I watch a movie, instead of concentrating on the film, I'm either busy jotting down phrases I *might* use some time, or I'm editing the script in my head.

"So why do you write at all?" you may ask. I've thought about that for a long, long time. The first answer that pops into my head lickety-split is always *Fulfillment!* On second thought that couldn't be right because fulfillment means fulfilling one's dreams, finding peace, contentment, reaching Nirvana. Marrying the best man in the whole world? Raising a family? Arriving at a restful, peaceful old age? Oh no. Not for me! Those choices are too simple for me.

Sometimes I hear writers say, "I feel—happy when I'm writing—so—fulfilled." If you ask me, that sentence needs revision. My advice to them is "Clichéd, unoriginal and derivative. Bring me the corrected copy!"

Perhaps now you see why I've never been pleased with any of my work and why I'm not likely to finish anything soon. Even if I take John McFee's advice and don't overdo it.

Oops! Sorry! I have to stop now. I need to call my sister and read her the first draft of this essay. Tomorrow, I'll work on draft #2.

The Perfect House

Elizabeth was astonished when her children asked what she wanted for her 70th birthday. Without blinking an eye she answered "I want us all to go away together to the seashore—for a week."

She knew that was a lot to ask. *I'm terrible*, she thought with a touch of shame. Then she quickly forgave herself. *But after all, when you get to be my age, it's OK to be a little selfish*. Without thinking and with a great flourish she announced, "*I'll* rent us a house. *You* can all wine and dine me."

Elizabeth had a small family. There was Jake, her first born, and Ezra who came bellowing into the world less than two years later. *Not much to show for myself*. As always, she forgave herself and with shoulders lifted, arms crossed over her belly, and chin high she harrumphed, *And I raised them all alone with no help from anybody*.

Later that day she realized she had made a rash, even stupid blunder. Counting on her fingers she calculated. "There's Jake and his gang, that's four, and Ezra's Boston crew, that's another four and then there's me. That makes nine people and that means five bedrooms. Not possible!" Somehow her small family had become a baseball team.

She tried counting another way. "There's two families and me. That should be three bedrooms. Jake and Nina can sleep in one. Ezra and Ruth can have another. The four kids can all squeeze in together—and then of course, there has to be one for me."

But that meant four bedrooms after all. What was the big difference between a four- and a five-bedroom house? The first was a very large "cottage" and rented for a small fortune. The second was a "summer family treasure" and was obscenely expensive. What the hell! In for a penny, in for a pound. A five-bedroom mansion it would be.

Since Elizabeth's birthday was in January they decided to celebrate after school closed in June. Calendars appeared, previous engagements and work schedules were examined and finally a week in mid-July was chosen.

The search began right after New Year's Day. You couldn't wait too long. Good houses were usually rented by last season's tenants. The others were grabbed up faster than you could say "Bob's yer uncle." Of course, a house that big would cost at least $4,000 for a week. She hoped she could find something cheaper.

Elizabeth answered one ad after another and was turned down one time after another. Some people didn't want children, some hadn't decided if they would rent or live in it, and others simply said "No".

At length she found an ad for a large house in Oyster Bay, a rich town on Long Island's North Shore facing Connecticut. Her friend Lois offered to be navigator on the way down. Lois was always helpful, cautious and extremely judgmental. If she saw anything she didn't like she would say, "This is unacceptable." All her friends would cringe. Nonetheless, if there was anything wrong that you might have missed, you could be sure Lois would find it.

After a dozen false starts, Elizabeth dialed a number and a friendly man's voice told her to come down and see it right away. It wasn't quite ready to be looked at yet because it was so early in the season, but he said to come down and look it over anyway.

It was a dreary day in early April. Still, the ride was easy and when the women arrived the sun came out and the countryside seemed so fresh Lois clapped her hands in approval. They drove down a long street lined with majestic old trees. In the summer, the leaves provided some cool shady spots where the silent trees let a touch of warm sunlight filter through. Fieldstone homes were hidden behind tall privet hedges. The sycamores and oaks, waking up from their long hibernation, faced forward onto the road to see who was coming and they looked backward down the sloping lawns to view the pure white sandy beach. *What a joy it will be to sink my toes into that sand—follow the flow of the white-capped waves. If a storm comes roaring in, those waves will rise up so high we'll have to run inside for safety.* Elizabeth longed to be there.

From a twist in the road they could see a slow moving river whose mouth opened to let the salt water enter and leave with the tides.

"I can't find the address. There should be a mailbox with the street number on it." Elizabeth was tired of the drive and frustrated by the bad directions she had.

"We just passed two mailboxes side by side."

"Well I hope it's the first driveway, the one on the right. The left one looks like a dirt road."

She made the U-turn and a robust, weather-beaten, smiling man appeared and waved them into his road—the one on the left. He was wearing a faded denim jacket with matching torn jeans below which heavy water-proof boots protruded. The friends looked at each other, alarmed. As Elizabeth stepped out of the car, she realized that her sensible walking shoes were a big mistake. She slid around in the mud and hung onto the car door, as a foul smell rose up to attack her.

Lois remained stuck firmly in the passenger seat. "This won't do at all. It is simply unacceptable."

"Let's look anyway. I want to see what you can get for $2,500."

Reluctantly, Lois stepped out of the car. Elizabeth was busy shaking the man's hand. He looked like a dirt farmer, not at all like a landlord, not even like a gentleman farmer. The stench engulfing her confirmed her worst fear.

"Hello ladies. How was your trip?"

"Oh, it was just fine. There wasn't too much traffic and the rain stopped half way here."

"Did you have any trouble finding this place?"

"Not too much."

"Well it's a *real* pleasure to meet you." His face cracked open into a welcoming smile. "I'll show you the inside later. The house isn't ready yet, so it's a little musty. See those two buildings? Yours is the big one closest to the river. Mine is the smaller one in the back. You can see it over there. If I stand at that kitchen door I can look straight into your house without any trouble at all. I like to check up and make sure that everything's alright."

Elizabeth, Lois, and John (as he was called) made their way through the pool of muddy water that separated both houses. They passed a rusty grill and a splintered redwood table without a single bench in sight.

"That grill's great for cookin'. We always set it up in June, so don't you worry about that. It's old but it works. My son and I, we share everything with our renters."

The stench grew stronger as they turned the corner and almost fell into a bunch of assorted chickens and hens. The birds flapped their flightless wings while an angry rooster rushed at Lois. Poor Lois. She wished she had never come.

John's speech kept shifting from college-educated English to backwater slang.

"Them hens is good layers. Just grab some eggs for breakfast if you feel like it. There's lots for all yours and mine." He paused proudly to see how that news went over. There was no response.

"Well, let's go down to the river. You can just get a peek at it from the front windows. That there's the master bedroom. I guess you two will be sharin' it?"

Lois shook her head and glanced back wistfully to the warm, safe car. The women cautiously picked their way down the overgrown path trying to keep their shoes from getting caught in the bushy roots. John plunged forward, safe in his muddy boots. They came to an empty river bed. Boats were strewn here and there caught in the mud, looking for all the world like beached whales. If you looked to the left you could see the river's mouth.

Their host explained expansively, "This here's called an estuary. When the tide's out it's a wet marshy place. Birds circle all the time tryin' to catch the bugs for dinner. When the tide turns, the ocean water backs in and the boats haul up and float. It's a fine place to canoe and kids love to swim here."

There were no birds. The flying insects hadn't arrived yet. It wasn't warm enough. But there was no doubt they would return. You could count on it. Moisture streamed down the barks of the overgrown trees. It was dark and damp; mosquitoes couldn't wait to breed here. Elizabeth had visions of males catching females in flight and mounting them from behind. *Do mosquitoes actually enjoy sex?* Elizabeth tried to remember how it used to be, but after all this time, it escaped her.

The odd trio walked towards the big house. Elizabeth stayed abreast of their guide; Lois trailed behind. Both women tried to avoid the chicken droppings and the aggressive rooster. A farm dog ran up barking. They were afraid he might bite them or, worse yet, greet them with muddy paws and sloppy wet kisses. The clucking and barking made a grand polyphonic chorale—like a concert without the comfort of velvet seats.

"I hope you like the place. It'll be ship-shape by the time you get here."

"It's a grand place," Elizabeth lied. "If the house is as nice as you say, it would be a wonderful place to spend a week."

"Well, I gotta fix the missin' stair for ya'. But for now, use that cinder block. It makes a pretty good step. I get a kick outta doin' my own work."

"I used to farm," he rambled on, "but then my bones started creakin', so I sold off most of the land. My rich neighbors, with their fancy mansions, would love to get rid of me. They can't abide the chickens and the dogs and the smells. They got a warrant once, but a lotta good it's done 'em. This here's my land and there ain't nothing they can do about it."

Lois looked at the makeshift stair, turned and started walking towards the car.

"My friend can't step that high," Elizabeth explained. "She has arthritis in her right knee so she'll just wait in the car."

With a deep intake of breath, Lois lifted her shoulders and peered imperiously over her glasses. "Well! I guess I can manage. I've come this far, I would like to see the inside of the house." She turned around with newfound determination, but with the strong conviction that "unacceptable" had become something worse. The only consolation was the story she would tell when her friends dropped in to schmooze.

Inside it was a disaster! They stepped into a long pantry with shelves too high to reach and too narrow for a can of beans. Rusty nails jutted out from mildewed walls.

"This here's the mud room. You leave your boots here on the floor and you hang your coats on those nails. Real handy, ain't it?"

The hall led into a kitchen the size of a squirrel's nest. A small table came within a hair's breadth of the walls. Its chipped surface peeked out from under a tattered tarpaulin.

"There's nine of you, right? I guess you won't all be eatin' together."

Next, a cursory look at the tiny living room. The windows faced east so the only view was the landlord's house.

"I would like to see the bedrooms now."

They trudged up an unlit narrow staircase, hugging the wall to keep from falling down the uneven steps. *Coming down will be worse*, Elizabeth thought. She pictured an ambulance, stretcher bearers struggling through the muck, years of wheelchairs and being fed through a straw. She smelled the hospital and the stink of the bedpan. She felt the hands of her caretaker moving noisily around the house, endlessly, until her final, lonely day.

The bedrooms were tiny. Moldy mattresses leaned against the walls of rooms that reeked of mildew. Something dead was rotting somewhere. The master bedroom had a fireplace which, John promised, would work once it was cleaned up. But, he added, they might not want to use it anyway.

"What's that yellow thing in the fireplace? It'll have to go before we get here."

"Oh, we always leave it there. It's only Styrofoam. It keeps the mosquitoes out. They come from the estuary. Ya' know?"

Elizabeth looked out the window at the ground below. She saw the path leading from the broken back steps down to the river's edge. She saw her grandchildren, squealing and laughing as they ran and tripped and giggled their way down to swim in the filthy water. Her dream was a nightmare.

"We better be moving on," she said. "We have some other things to see, but this is a marvelous house and I'll have to bring my sons to see it."

John chuckled. "I know. Lots'a people say that when they're leaving. But it don't matter much. There's this nice family from upstate New York. They like to come down here every summer just to see the water. They don't get to see it much up there."

John waved and smiled at them as they were leaving. The car backed out onto the smooth, paved street.

On the way out of town, Elizabeth and Lois stopped at a cozy inn, had hot soup, crusty brown bread and a cup of tea. They laughed all the way home.

Barnes & Noble

"Bargain Books—Greatly Reduced—An Extra 10% off for Members." The signs are magnetic forces pulling customers inexorably toward the imposing displays. Men and women pick up over-sized books, fondle them, feel the smooth pages, linger over the images. They choose a few and sit by the windows where the sunlight illuminates the pages. Or they take them to the café where they sit over cups of cappuccino enjoying the prose while the sweet aroma of cinnamon and chocolate surrounds them.

Take a closer look.

Watch the people drawn to other places, wild spaces near the towering Rocky Mountains with valleys down below. They taste the wild strawberries, hear the rushing water, smell the honeysuckles, feel the soft meadow grass under foot.

There a newborn fawn is lying on the ground as the doe gently raises him on wobbly legs to taste his mother's milk. They hear majestic lions roar. They touch the lamb's furry shawl. They smell the cedars in the swamp.

Then, they look at the prices, sigh, and take these treasures home to be placed on shelves to join other books of a wondrous world full of untouched places and fantastic animals. They might never look at the pictures again, but those images are theirs to keep.

A different breed of buyers arrive. They gravitate to the games and jigsaw puzzles, Black Belt Sudoku and NY Times Crossword Puzzle books. They rummage through the shelves looking for any new Acrostics that are never there.

The gamesters don't sit and savor their finds. They hide them under some great classic—"Pride and Prejudice," "Chaucer's Tales," "The Rise and Fall of the Roman Empire". Each teetering stack moves to checkout and the customer blushes when the cashier examines each item one by one.

The gift shoppers! Should it be journals, or calendars? Perhaps a cookbook or scented candles? Do they really need fancy matching wrappings and shopping bags? Don't forget the birthday card, anniversary card, get well card. Maybe it's time for the grandchildren's gifts. "Babar" or "Pinkalicious" or "Curious George" for the little ones. "Harry Potter" or "Goosebumps" for the older kids. Maybe the Beatles or Madonna for the teenagers. Whatever they choose, they rush out the door so as not to miss the festivities.

Here come the truly elite, the crème de la crème. First come the music aficionados who strut to the rear in search of CDs. On their heels come the movie lovers rushing to the DVDs. Both are seeking great works of art. The music lovers shiver with delight to find something that somehow was lost over time. Bernstein conducting his own "Requiem" or Benjamin Britain's "Ceremony of Carols". Film buffs look for original versions of classic movies. "Psycho" with Anthony Perkins or "Sleuth" with Laurence Olivier and the young Michael Caine. Orson Welles' tawny Othello. Both shoppers walk out looking disdainfully at the ordinary folks wandering aimlessly through the aisles. As they leave, they guard their purchases as if they were relics from a distant and better culture.

Of course, there are the people who still remember that Barnes & Noble was always, first and foremost, a bookstore. Each person has a special interest, a unique taste. Some choose mystery and romance. Some like fiction and memoirs. Others choose poetry, religion, history, biography, science, psychology or self-help. One shopper will only look at the hard covers while the man next to him will only examine the trade paperbacks so he can conserve space in his own library.

So they stare at the countless variety of books, each book vying for the perfect space to catch a book lover's eye. And the overjoyed, perplexed readers stand amazed, mouth agape, eyes scanning the row upon row of shelves, from the first book too high to reach to the last title too low to read.

In the end, piles of secret treasures move out the door to be placed lovingly on shelves and coffee tables and end tables and night tables and stacks on the floor. The contented Barnes & Noble shoppers smile. They are happiest in the midst of all their own special clutter.

Nature vs. Nurture

Everyone has fears. It's in your genes. Ancient forebears passed it down to their children and their children's children, even unto the end of time. The way I figure it, if you have a gene for something like cancer or over-eating or gambling, it's in your DNA—a hidden weapon of mass destruction waiting to zap you, crush you like a bug.

If you have a troublesome gene, you might not even know it. It lies dormant until something wakes it up and it knocks you flat on your ass. If life is simple, that gene stays asleep. It's like, if you never kiss a boy, you'll never catch a cold, right?

My father gave me his DNA for acrophobia. That condition causes extreme fear of heights. I was born with a propensity for the disease, but it never caught up with me until I was about eight years old. Here's how it happened.

My father couldn't look down from an open window or lift a foot onto a ladder. It was his daughters who put up the screens in the spring and took them down again in the fall. He stood below and gave directions.

My father took us to Niagara Falls. We went to look down. He turned yellowish green. We got in the elevator and looked up from the bottom. We never got a good look. We just got wet.

My father needed a bath to wash away the sweat every time he drove over the Brooklyn Bridge.

The first symptom of my acrophobia was a subset fear called lifta-phobia activated by the sight of elevators. Open elevator cages let me see flimsy cables as I was carried over empty deadly spaces. Glass box elevators afforded panoramic views growing smaller as I rose quickly over empty deadly spaces. Pretty soon you simply said, "elevator" or "lift" and I sensed empty deadly spaces.

My first husband thought he could cure me. He took me to high places: the top of the Eiffel Tower in Paris, the Wasserturm in Mannheim, and the edge of a cliff overlooking the Rhine. Wherever we went, he would encourage me. "Look down! Look down!" he would cry. He finally gave up on a trip to the Catskills to enjoy the fall foliage. He took the ski lift to see the golden forests. I stayed below to see the dying grass.

My second husband thought I was perfect when we got married, which of course, led to a new fear, divorce-a-phobia, the precipitating cause of which is experience.

On our honeymoon in the Virgin Islands we wandered through Charlottesville on a road that rose gently to the top of a hill. We rested a while and looked out. His spine tilted forward. Mine formed a thirty degree angle—backwards. It was time to go. The path on that sweet slope was too slow. By chance there was a long, unbroken staircase leading down to the front of our idyllic hideaway. "We'll take the stairs," he said. "It's much faster."

Sotto voce I replied, *I'm sure it is. It will take me a mere fifteen seconds to reach the bottom.*

"No choice," he said and he began trotting down.

My God! Married only forty-eight hours, and we're having our first fight and this one I can't win! I flopped down on the top of that hell bound road and descended all eighty-seven steps, one by one—on my butt.

Years later when the honeymoon was over, I realized our sweet marriage turned sour that very night. As the sun set over the azure sea, my husband returned to his romantic mood. He lovingly raised my nightgown, peeled it over my head, drew me to the bed, and playfully rolled me over. A shriek rang out, the moment lost. My bruised swollen backside shone in the dark like the rump of a randy baboon.

As the ardor died, so did our love. Looking for help we found and shared a therapist—a mistake of monumental proportions. She saw our problem as black and white. I was black and he was white. And I'm not talking rear ends here.

So now I have a new fear—the fear of all things psychiatric. She and I parted and I found a therapist I could call my own. He couldn't cope with my latest fear, so he decided to fix an old one. He suggested we hold our sessions riding up and down in a glass enclosed elevator for the whole forty-five minute hour. He said it would help to go to Coney Island, first ride the Ferris wheel and then graduate to the Parachute Jump. At each suggestion, I twisted and squirmed and whimpered. He *did* manage to have me climb up onto his desk and look down at the floor while he steadied me with his hand. Then he let go. I was left standing on an oak desk, a weeping willow planted there forever until a strong wind uprooted me and I would fall to my sad, but inevitable end.

That didn't work so I left.

I never have gotten over my acrophobia. I get panic attacks at the mention of height. They are assaults ranging from skirmishes to Armageddon if I miss my daily Klonopin.

Over the years other DNA problems grabbed hold. The terrors came and went. Fear of going outside followed by fear of staying inside. Fear of the dark but fear of too much light. But above all, the fear that I might be stupid enough to marry again. These failures are forever with me. Even when I think I'm cured, I'm only in remission.

I inherited so many fears from my father's side but I can't even count the ones my mother's DNA passed on.

So Here's the Thing . . .

So here's the thing. It's four o'clock in the morning and I just woke up and I had this dream and I had to get up and write it down as if I were in analysis or something.

Let me tell you, I've been having this really bad back pain like you don't know if it will kill you but you know it can't be serious because everyone says a little water walking will make it better. So I've been moaning and groaning and telling people how bad it is but don't worry it can't be cancer like my ex-husband had when they told him it was only sciatica.

To get to the point, I've been taking hot showers and walking a lot and when that wasn't any good I've been sitting a lot but that made it worse because my knee's been crooked ever since that bicycle accident I had when I was twelve, the one that laid me up for a whole summer with water on the knee as if I were an Irish washerwoman down on all fours scrubbing the floors all day.

Anyway, sleeping is very complicated because I'm pushing seventy-two and sleeping isn't my strong suit, what with those post-menopausal aches and pains that doctors always tell me I should consider myself lucky because I never had any hot flashes or night sweats or anything. But you know—even if it wasn't for a back that might seize up and kill me—even if everyone says it's nothing and I pamper myself too much— even if they say I should get some exercise even if I hate water walking—or I should at least sit on a chair and raise weights over my head to build some upper body strength which I'll probably need when I get my walker. Even if it wasn't all that—sleeping is still very complicated.

To get back to tonight, I couldn't lay on my left side and the right side was worse. The pain in the right side of my back is way, way down, so I don't have to tell you it's a real pain in the ass and you can imagine I have a lot of trouble getting to sleep.

Well, you know how when you get to be seventy-two if you drink too much water you wake up all night to go pee? And the ladies on the bench in Prospect Park tell you, "Are you crazy or something? You can't drink after six or you'll be up all night peeing," and I say "Yeah, yeah," ya' know?

So anyway, sleep is a big thing and with a pain in the butt like mine, lying down in a bed with a trough in the middle "ain't no bed a' roses", I'm telling you! So I lower myself very slowly onto the edge of the sunken mattress and wait to see if my bones are still where they should be, and when I know for *sure* that they're only crooked and not broken I either slowly raise my legs and swizzle around real gentle like and rest my head on the pillow, or I do the legs and swizzle thing in a single quick twist like I was some kind of athlete in the Barnum & Bailey Circus. But it doesn't matter which thing I do because if I do the trapeze artist thing I yell for God to give me a break and if I do the twist and turn thing I scream "Holy

Jesus, Mother of God!" which is really funny because I'm not Irish and I'm not even Catholic!

Well, last night I decided to try the raise and swizzle maneuver. You see I've been doing all the walking or not-walking, and all the sitting or not-sitting—but not the laying on the bed. Because if you have a really mean back and you lay down it just makes everything worse and getting up feels like a rhinoceros is stomping on your back so I just lay there on my crummy mattress and decided never to get up again. What I was really wishing for was for some big strong male nurse to come in and scoop me up in his arms and I'd never ever have to move again.

Well, "that's neither here nor there," as my mother used to say.

Yesterday was a good day and I could bend real well, so I don't worry and I brush my teeth, and I get into my bed that sags so much it looks like a trench and not a bed that could hold your bones in place and keep them from shaking around. And I feel my back attacking from the rear, so to speak, and I shout "Shit!" Still, I keep my wits about me, like they say, 'cause I figure if I keep my wits about me in a circle I'll figure out how to get out of the damn circle somehow.

Now, you've got to understand that I took this Stress Reduction Program which is really a way of saying meditation without scaring people away—because I'm a nervous wreck and my son said that it would make me feel better. That's my son, The Doctor. So I went to this meeting for five weeks and it was snowing and when it wasn't snowing I couldn't park my beat up blue Honda because all the spaces were full of mountains of disgusting dirty snow. When I got there I did all the stuff they said and I meditated sitting, I meditated standing, I meditated lying on the floor, walking around a table and I ate one damn raisin for five minutes. So I tried as hard as I could but my son and I knew all along that it was a big waste of time because with or without it I'm going to die real soon anyway.

Anyway, last night I got into bed and I thought I'd just try that stuff and maybe I'll relax and the cat won't crowd me off the bed like she can do when she's feeling super chummy. The way this thing works is, you don't think about anything and you relax all the parts of your body starting from your head to your jaw past your neck and your chest, through your abdomen and your gentles, down your thighs and legs and out the bottom of your toes until all that nervousness seeps out into the bed and you feel as calm as a clam.

So I start doing my stress reduction thing and I'm feeling OK but when I get to my back I'm feeling like just one big blob of back pain and I'm feeling like shit, so I concentrate very, very hard and I "work my way through it" like those midwives on PBS say all the time—and the pain goes away and I whisper "Thank you, whoever you are, thank you," because both my right hip and my left knee feel good at the same time. So, I smile and go on with my exercises knowing that now they will put me to sleep.

But here's the thing—when I do this imaging thing I'm OK through the jaw and the neck and straight through the abdomen but it's the gentles part that's the problem.

I can't just lie there and try to feel my gentles and relax them because the minute I do they just tense up and there ain't no way I can move past them to get to my thighs. So I'm lying there and I'm trying to relax but instead I get all tense and while I'm trying to go to sleep, instead I'm just sort of lying there moaning and groaning. No matter how hard I try it just gets worse and worse and I start moaning and groaning to beat the band along with some squealing and thrashing around and the cat jumps up next to me and looks at me closely, and I try to push her away so as not to break the spell but she starts making those obscene advances on my pillow.

By this time my mind is going blank and I am *completely* in the moment and before you can say "Bob's yer uncle," I am fast asleep.

Now here's the funny part. I had this weird dream like I was playing a game with that kid I see in Prospect Park and it's the game where you have these little plastic pieces that are cars and trucks and motorcycles and ambulances and you have to get your parked car out of these tight parking spots without crashing into the other cars. But it turns out the cars are really logs and the logs are really pretzels rods and I have to get them to line up perfectly so I can make a pretzel raft and I could use it to go to—and I wake up!

I wake up but it don't make any sense and I'm swearing and muttering because I *got* that pretzel raft together and I want to know what came next.

So I roll over and get up and take a pee and I ain't moaning or groaning, not even one little peep. Then I get back into bed without that noisy part and don't even notice that the pain is gone away. When I realize what happened I can't believe it but I figure it was the gentles thing that cured me so I got some first class sleep and I just dozed right off into Dreamland and it didn't even matter if I was pushing seventy-two, I knew exactly how to fall asleep again even in the middle of the night after a fucking dream.

Well I had to get up and write this all down and it's already six o'clock and my pillow beckons but I'm wide awake and ready to face the world even "until Hell freezes over," like my mother used to say.

But I've been sitting here scrunched over this pad for a couple of hours scribbling with my dull number two pencil and feeling like some kind of hotshot, but I have to get up and take two Extra Strength Tylenol. My back is killing me.

My Red A-Line Dress

I was sitting in front of Gate 7C in the JFK terminal on a Wednesday night in August. It was 9:00 p.m. and the place was usually quiet by then, but that night there were a few women and one man sitting there waiting for the non-stop flight to El Paso. I was wearing my red A-line dress because my shrink said A-lines were the best thing for my body type. American Airline's "red-eye" was scheduled to take off at 10:00 p.m. I prayed for the plane to leave on time or my red eyes would be scarlet by the time we arrived. I needed to stay up all night because I knew that a plane traveling 30,000 feet up in the stratosphere would never make it to New Jersey let alone to Texas.

This particular over-night flight was also known as the red-eye because it landed in El Paso, the first stop on the way to Juarez to get a Quickie Mexican Divorce. That explained the large number of women at the airport. Men don't rush to Mexico very often and if they do, they never shed a tear.

On the Monday of that week, my Brooklyn Court Street Lawyer had received "Power of Attorney" from my soon-to-be-ex-husband and passed it along to his contact lawyer in El Paso. Over the phone, I had to choose grounds for divorce so all the paper work I needed would be ready for Tuesday. I chose "incompatibility" which was a little strange after a 6-year courtship and a 12-year marriage. I toyed with the idea of "cruel and inhuman treatment" but my ex never gave me so much as a bloody nose, and *everyone* gets agita from long relationships. Adultery was appropriate, but orchestrating a scenario in some two-bit hotel would take too much time and was too sleazy.

On Tuesday morning I went to Court Street again to sign my Petition for Divorce. It was in English so I knew what I was signing. There was also a round-trip ticket to fly American Airlines flight 666 to El Paso the next night. Tuesday night was fully booked. While I was there, my Brooklyn Lawyer gave me instructions and said not to worry about finding my El Paso Lawyer because *that* lawyer would find *me*. When I left the office I had my papers, my tickets and a silent prayer that my soon-to-be-ex wouldn't suddenly change his mind and rescind his Power of Attorney. The bastard was good at dirty tricks.

On Wednesday night, at the airport we waited impatiently to board the plane. It left JFK a quarter of an hour after midnight setting a record for the shortest delay for an overnight special on any American Airlines flight. We arrived safely early Thursday morning. I sat up all night playing gin rummy with a man who was on his way home from a business trip. We drank gin and tonic, chatted and played cards all the way, probably because I looked so good in my red A-line dress that was perfect for my body type. He was not wearing a ring. I was charming and made a lot of witty jokes. When we landed he took my phone number and I thought *All I have to do is wear an A-line dress and I'll be set.*

I checked into the airport hotel, washed my face, put on fresh lipstick, brushed off my wrinkled red A-line dress, noticed how it enhanced my body type and by 7:00 a.m. I was sitting in the hotel lobby. At one end of the lobby was a door, wooden on the bottom and frosted glass on top. It reminded me of the scene in "The Maltese Falcon" where a door like that opens into an empty room with Humphrey Bogart sitting with his feet up on the desk waiting for the phone to ring. It also reminded me of the doors in P.S. 152 in Brooklyn behind which old teachers in sensible laced-up shoes tormented us with poetry and grammar.

A young girl came through the door, approached three women and me, collected our papers and exited through the same door, popping her gum as she went. Soon my El Paso Lawyer appeared and strode across the lobby wearing a shabby blue suit, a bright red tie and a cowboy hat. He looked like a movie extra by the way he marched up to greet us with a smile so wide we could see his molars. One woman in the group had a man with her and the two whispered and giggled the whole the time. Another woman was crying. I wondered why, if she was *that* unhappy, why she would rush down to El Paso to get a Quickie Mexican Divorce, especially considering that she would have to fly 30,000 feet up in the stratosphere to get there. She did it because her husband refused to give her any alimony if she didn't.

I couldn't even think about alimony because my soon-to-be-ex didn't have any money anyway. I *did* ask for the house we bought when I was working for nine years and he was out walking the dog and meeting "God knows who". I demanded the house, custody of our two sons, $25 a week child support, plus health and dental insurance for the kids that he got free from his NYC teachers' benefit plan. It was a sweetheart deal. He signed it.

The cowboy asked if any of us planned to get married that day. If so, he would speed up the process and prepare the wedding for the same afternoon. Of course, that would cost extra. The giggling couple whispered in each other's ears and nodded. He explained that we were no longer divorce seekers but were petitioners and then he told us to follow him out. We formed a line and followed him like lemmings rushing to follow their leader and run off the edge of a cliff. I felt like I was back in the schoolyard when the bell rang as the signal to hurry up, get in line in size order and march back into school.

We followed the cowboy to a small van and we all managed to squeeze in. The driver sped from the hotel and before we could say, "Frankly my dear, I don't give a damn," we were at the end of a long line of cars at the U.S. border in El Paso, waiting to cross the Mexican border into Juarez. Armed guards were everywhere, asking people to step out of their cars, hand over their papers, open their trunks, and answer a few questions. Some people took back their papers, closed their trunks, got back in their cars and moved on. Others closed their trunks, got back in their cars, gave up their papers and drove to the end of another line where there were more armed guards. They waited on that line until they were escorted into a trailer, perhaps never to be seen again.

My nervous little group had passports, there was nothing in the trunk (at least I hoped not) and we were ready to jump out to answer any questions they asked. It looked like everything was OK, but I was scared anyway. "A Touch of Evil" with Charlton Heston and Janet Leigh flashed through my mind. They had raced over the border into Mexico where they met Marlene Dietrich and Orson Welles and unspeakable things happened to them.

A guard with his gun in his holster came to our car, glanced at the driver, nodded to the cowboy and waved us on our way from the U.S. border to a spot a few yards away. The Mexican border guard waved us into Juarez without so much as a "Fare Thee Well". A border guard could get very rich collecting money from people eager for Quickie Mexican Divorces and from sleazy mustachioed men who never had to open their trunks. Sometimes a guard was lucky and collected twice from the same car crossing and re-crossing the border on the same day.

As we got out of the van in front of the courthouse in Juarez, I brushed off my red A-line dress that complimented my body type. We were greeted by other petitioners, each group with its own cowboy lawyer. They sat us down on narrow wooden benches. We were all sweating, watching flies buzz half-heartedly around squeaky ceiling fans. We saw the flies swarm and the blades turn but it did absolutely nothing to cool us off.

We faced an enormous desk where a tiny judge sat behind giant stacks of legal documents. The first stack was on his right. It was the in-pile. The stack was so high I thought all the papers would crash down and suffocate him just like those newspapers did to the Collier Brothers in New York. These were the petitions waiting for the judge's decision. It was always the same. Judgment in favor of the plaintiff. Proof that the "Grounds for Divorce" was really irrelevant. The pile on his left contained the approved petitions that carried the judge's signature.

The judge followed a pattern of movements so well-choreographed it was like a ballet. He stood up, took a petition from the top of the pile on his right, sat down, signed the petition, leaned over and put the document on top of the left pile. When that pile got too high, an old man shuffled over and took it away. The judge rose again to repeat the maneuver. The system provided exercise and job security for both the judge and the old man because there was a never-ending supply of petitions.

There was a third stack of papers by the door where we had come in. Each time a lawyer entered he slid his clients' petitions under the bottom of that pile. At the exact moment the judge reached into his in-pile, a Spanish-speaking official picked up a petition from this third pile and called someone to the desk. Then, the official announced the petitioner's name, the judge looked up, nodded, looked down and continued his endless dance.

When I was called to the desk the judge nodded at me. I signed my petition thereby swearing that I had lived in Mexico for the last six months and requesting a divorce on the grounds of incompatibility. The official slid my petition on the bottom of the un-signed pile. It would reach the top by Friday morning and then I would actually have my Quickie Mexican Divorce. It would be mailed to me on Monday. My Brooklyn Lawyer had already sent the postage and handling fee to the Texas Lawyer. The efficiency was staggering.

When it was all over, I wasn't quite sure what I had signed because it was all in Spanish. I wondered if I had confessed to a vicious crime or maybe enlisted in the Mexican Army. Our

El Paso Lawyer nodded to us and it was all over in a New York minute.

I stood up, still wearing my red A-line dress that just suited my body type, and once again we all squeezed into the sweaty van. The driver made a quick stop at a souvenir shop in Juarez and waited while we shopped. Then he took us back to the hotel in time to pick up the next batch of petitioners.

Each of us bought a souvenir to remember that remarkable day. Back at the hotel, we checked out and went to the bar to have a few drinks while we waited for the noon flight back home. We were patient while the staff of American Airlines flight 777 cleaned up the mess left by the sloppy passengers from Los Angeles. We boarded the plane at half past one which was a one and a half hour delay. Not too bad compared to the flight from New York which left two and a quarter hours late. Maybe American Airlines had improved since the day before.

Some people had bought Mexican sandals. Some had bought silver candelabras and sweet, sticky candies. I bought an orange and black poncho to replace the faithful red A-line dress even though the poncho would never compliment my body type.

I wore that orange and black poncho until I got my Dominican Republic Divorce. My second ex-husband flew down and, as far as I know, he never brought back a souvenir. I started calling my first husband my ex-minus-one. My most recent ex forgot that trip as soon as he married his ridiculously young girlfriend and sired two daughters and moved to the suburbs where they all lived happily ever after.

I gave up my orange and black poncho and, though I can't say I lived happily ever after, I gladly gave my second ex-husband to his third wife.

Tyler and Schuyler

"Don't worry," Hilda told Cindy, "he'll tell you what he wants. I gotta run now or I'll be late for the podiatrist." Mrs. Johnson waddled out the door, weighed down by her 8-month pregnant belly, her feet obviously in need of some TLC.

"OK Mrs. J. Don't worry about a thing." Cindy turned to Tyler. "Let's play a game. First, let's take that Binky out of your mouth so I can understand you." He was sucking on a big plastic disc that covered his face from his chin to just under his nose.

Tyler shook his head furiously. Cindy reached for the pacifier. Tyler pushed it out with his tongue and roared, "Tyler's paddy-faddy!" Imperiously, he popped the disgusting wet thing back in his mouth. Then he looked around for his mother.

"Mommy had to go out but she'll be back soon. She's got a boo-boo on her toe and the Doctor will fix it."

Tyler's raised just his left eyebrow. "Meemee's cobbies?"

Cindy was stumped, but, undaunted she pushed bravely on. "Mommy went out for just a little while. I bet she'll bring back something very special just for you. She'll go to the store, right?"

"Soo Mock? Meemee's pocky-co?"

A deadly chill ran up then down Cindy's spine, through her legs, into her toes and leaked out onto the floor. She shivered with fear. She hadn't understood one word, since "paddy faddy." What had Hilda been thinking? "He'll let you know." *Help me*, Cindy prayed. *Lord, help me,* she moaned. There was no exit, no escape. There was no fairy godmother or kindly angel to lead the way. Only a miracle could help her now.

Suddenly, a ray of sunshine burst through the gloom. Cindy looked around and there on the desk was the pad Hilda had left. The happy baby sitter jumped up, laughing with relief. She was completely penniless, she really needed this job. Mrs. J had left "A Dictionary of Tyler Words". Everything would be OK. *Thank you, thank you Hilda!* Cindy read out loud:

TYLER'S SPECIAL WORDS
Paddy-faddy = Pacifier (sometimes called Binky)
Soo Mock = Super Market
Pocky-co = Pocketbook
Banny-bunna = Bannister
Cobbies = corn on the cob or corns on your feet
Wawas = flowers

"OK Ty, let's read." She picked a book that had a big smiling bear on the cover. "What about this one?"

"*Zentle Ziant?*" Tyler asked, shook his head and brought her a much-read book with a faded cover. It was his favorite, "Ferdinand the Bull".

It was Cindy's favorite too and she read it out loud with love and compassion for the charming beast. She began to read. Every time she came to the part where it said, "He sat under the cork tree and—" Tyler would clap his hands and shout "Mell dee wawas!" Cindy roared with laughter. She couldn't stop. Tears ran down her cheeks. She really loved this. She wouldn't mind taking Tyler home with her, he was so adorable.

After books and blocks, Cindy put Tyler in his crib for his afternoon nap. He hugged the spotted dog waiting there for him, yawned and stuck his pacifier in his mouth. His sheet was decorated with teddy bears and balloons. He rolled over on his belly, tucked his knees under him, and made himself comfortable with his bottom stuck up in the air. Cindy hummed a few bars of "Hush Little Baby" and his eyes fluttered. As they closed in sleep he smiled and the pacifier fell out of his mouth.

This is marvelous, she thought. Tyler was irresistible. He had soft sandy colored hair, chubby cheeks and rosy lips. When he was born he was blessed with big brown eyes, so dark for a little baby. And now they sparkled with joy and surprise as he toddled through his new bright world.

After a couple of peaceful hours, Cindy heard a murmur from the bedroom. She went in. Tyler was holding the crib bars, and was jumping up and down waving his pacifier in the air. When he saw her, he beamed so brightly she practically cried.

"Are you thirsty, Ty?" she asked as she removed his soaked Huggies and fastened a fresh one around his bulging belly. His eyes opened wide. He nodded his head vigorously. "Tyler tirsty," he agreed.

Tyler took her hand and dragged Cindy to the kitchen. She opened the fridge door and he pointed joyously to a baby bottle full of Hawaiian Punch. He couldn't give up his bottle any more than he could relinquish his pacifier.

He drank rapturously. "You really love that drink don't you? Does your mommy like it too?"

Without missing a single tug on the alarmingly real looking nipple, Tyler shook his head slowly from side to side.

"What does your mommy like? What's her favorite drink?"

Tyler thought a while. Then, "A tup of key!" he squealed.

Just then the door opened and Hilda walked in wearily, bravely trying to smile. A little red truck stuck out of the paper bag perched on the ledge of her swollen stomach. Tyler turned, rushed up to his mother, grabbed her leg and crushed it to his chest with a big, warm, happy hug. He looked adoringly into her face.

"Meemee," he shouted. "Meemee home!"

Hilda dragged herself to the sofa, sat down and fell back exhausted. Her pregnant belly pushed her deep into the couch while her legs remained stuck to the floor by the relentless gravitational pull. "I feel like a piece of Turkish Taffy," she said and raised her legs, sighed, and turned to look at Ty.

"Do you want to see what meemee brought you?" Tyler grabbed the bag to see his new treasure. He pulled it out, squealed and gave the little red truck a push that sent it crashing into the wall where it got stuck underneath the radiator. Hilda groaned. She grabbed the back of the couch and tried to hoist herself up onto her swollen, weary legs.

"Don't worry, Mrs. J. I'll get it."

Cindy fetched the truck and kept Tyler with her while she tidied up the house. He was getting tired again, so she put him back in bed for another nap. She knew it wasn't a very good idea. He would be up 'til all hours that night.

By the time she came back to the living room, Mrs. Johnson was snoring lightly. Cindy thought about waking her and asking for her money, but didn't quite have the heart for it. Instead, she put on her jacket and quietly slipped out the front door.

As soon as she hit the cool air, she forgot about Tyler and Mrs. Johnson and binkies and diapers and Hawaiian Punch. She danced off to meet her boyfriend for hamburgers and fries at MacDonald's.

It was almost two years later when Cindy came back to babysit for Mrs. Johnson. This time she had two boys to take care of and her pay had been increased proportionately. In the intervening years she had seen Hilda in the playground with Tyler and she had even taken care of him from time to time. The babysitter had been around when Tyler started to talk big-people talk but he still had trouble with his *"G"* and called his book *"Curious Zeorze"* and chimed in *"Zames Zames Morrison Morrison"* when anyone read from his special A.A. Milne poetry book. Over time, Cindy saw Hilda begin to glow, then groan, then waddle.

When Hilda's water broke two months early, Cindy rose to the challenge. She rushed to Tyler's bedside at midnight and looked out the window as her boss struggled into the back seat of a taxi. Mrs. J had a smile on her face. *I don't have to be pregnant anymore,* she sighed as she squeezed into the tight space. She hadn't decided on a name for the baby yet. She didn't even know if it was a boy or a girl. During her short, unexpected labor she told the nurse, "I'm going to open up this newspaper and any name I see, that'll be it!" She opened the latest issue of the New York Times Sunday Magazine Section to a glossy ad for Johnnie Walker Black! Quickly shutting the paper, she returned to her appointed task and concentrated on her contractions.

After a while Cindy came back to babysit on a regular basis. Tyler was a nursery school dropout. On his first day at school, the teacher told everyone to lie down and rest. She turned to Tyler, plucked his pacifier from his mouth and put it in his cubby. That deft maneuver was the kiss of death. Tyler went back twice more and then, when the school mini-bus arrived on the fourth day, he planted his feet firmly on the top step of the stoop and refused to go. Instead, he stayed home every day to torment his baby brother. "I don't share!" he shouted and snatched the baby's toys away even if they happened to be rattles or teething rings.

It had taken Tyler eighteen months to learn to walk. When he was two and a half he gave up his diapers after he was bribed with a new teddy bear. But he wouldn't part with his favorite blue "paddy faddy". He was engaged to Becky whom he met in the sandbox. She was three months older than he was and the two mothers knew it was love at first sight when Tyler gave Becky his extra shovel and Becky stopped drizzling sand onto Tyler's head.

Becky's mom sighed. "I hope she stops wetting the bed by the time they get married."

"I hope she doesn't mind marrying someone with no teeth and very little hair," Hilda replied.

They sat and stared at their progeny and were content as they shared visions of weddings and grandchildren. But it all seemed too far away and they doubted they would ever live that long.

Schuyler learned to walk in a startling manner. Hilda was playing with the boys when the baby crawled over to the ottoman. He pulled himself up, banged on the stool with his pudgy fists and let go. Then, he teetered on his toes, caught his balance and took his first tentative steps—backwards. He took two or three more steps in reverse, plopped down on his rump and laughed out loud. Hilda shrieked with laughter. Tyler sulked. His reign of terror was over. Schuyler's backward walk continued for a whole week. If he wanted anything, he turned around and backed into it. With a rapid and proficient movement he turned and snatched it up before Tyler noticed.

Months grew into a year and then another six months dragged by. Schuyler pranced forward now. He walked like a pro, but still always glancing back to make sure his big brother was out of pouncing range. But he didn't speak. Not one word. Hilda began to wonder if something was amiss. Her sister would shake her head knowingly and mention to her friends that Schuyler had this oversized head from birth.

It was a Friday afternoon and Mrs. J had gone to meet a friend for some much-needed R&R. She had learned, soon enough, that raising two boys was not twice the effort of raising one. It increased by a factor of three or even four.

Tyler was getting cranky and Schuyler was sitting on the potty in the middle of the living room not knowing quite what to do but well aware that he always got attention that way. Cindy decided a little food might do the trick so she led the boys into the kitchen. Tyler climbed into his training chair. Cindy plopped smiling, silent Schuyler into his high chair.

She went to the closet to find a special treat. "Who wants a pretzel?" she whispered. From nowhere a new voice rang out, loud and clear, "Ah do!"

And that's how Schuyler finally began to speak. Mommy and Daddy weren't home to hear it, but they realized that their little one had conquered a brand new skill. Within days Schuyler was talking in sentences and by the end of two weeks he spoke in clear, distinct paragraphs. He was completely articulate while his brother was still saying "Let's go play on the Zungle Zim."

Tyler and Schuyler grew up fighting and squabbling and one-upping each other whenever they could. But sometimes, every now and then, they slept in the same room—in the same bed. Mr. and Mrs. Johnson worried about their kids' inability to accept each other. They sighed. Would it ever end?

But not to worry, the boys quit all that nonsense and learned to openly love each other. It only took thirty years.

Two Ways to Look at Color

Necessary Changes

Barbara and Mark came yesterday to see how my apartment looked now that I had it re-done.

Just a few years ago I bought this place. I found it, oddly enough, on a rainy Saturday afternoon when I was fooling around on my computer. It would be great, I thought, to get out of Avon and move to West Hartford. So I played around and surfed and sighed but nothing popped up. So I went to Craig's List and there I found *my place*. It was big, bright, dramatic, breath taking. I had to see it!

As I entered, all I could see was a shining mahogany floor that seemed to fill the air with the smell of dark chocolate. It stretched seamlessly from one end of the apartment to the other. Meg and Nick were sorry to leave this place. They were proud of their mahogany floor and the new rosewood kitchen cabinets and the black marbleized bathroom counters. They had an enormous couch that filled the majestic living room. It was a white leather sofa that demanded attention as it rested on the rich brown floor. In front of the sofa lay an Oriental rug that Meg had lovingly brought from her home in India.

And there were windows everywhere. The bedroom windows faced east, the morning sun streamed in promising golden days. The living room and dining room windows faced south. Warm afternoon light poured in through the quiet comforting windows. There was one special window where you could sit and see the sky and trees and birds circling high above. The place was irresistible, overwhelming—seductive.

I lived here for over a year and looked around carefully pondering how Meg and Nick had chosen this unusual decorator design. The mahogany colored floor turned out to be some kind of laminate with a high gloss finish. It was a mirror. I could see my image from below—an appalling sight. I could see the floor's scratches and every speck of dust that fluttered down and settled itself for the day.

Each room was painted a different color. Actually, each room was painted with a lack of color. One was slate grey, another a grayish-tinged blue and the hallways were a half-grey and half-beige white. The windowless kitchen with its dark cabinets was painted brown. The only color in the whole place was in the small bathroom. It was a vibrant royal blue. I could see in my mind the fun they must have had there.

After just a few months, a lucky thing happened. The mahogany floor began to come apart. I didn't notice it at first when the boards began to separate. Each morning I moved as quickly as I could to start my day with a cup of coffee. And each day, as I walked barefoot towards the kitchen, I felt a new space open under my toes. I heard the floors creak. What happened? It was brand new. Nick told me he had put it down slowly with infinite patience and care. Meg said it broke her heart to leave this floor behind.

I asked the handyman how it could be fixed and he simply shook his head. I called in my trusty contractor. He said it had to be replaced. My heart sank but at the same time, my spirits soared at the thought that I wouldn't have to look at it anymore. Pretty soon my toes began to trip on the ever-widening spaces and I could put my finger into each gaping crevice. I knew I had to make a decision.

What to do? Simple.

Down came the brown drapes with their bronze metallic rods. Up came the evil floor with it cracks and scratches. Out went the dull baseboards and ancient metal doors. And out went Tootsie and I, abandoning our home to let the workers do their magic.

The new oak floor had light and dark earth tones. Wooden closets and doors were a gentle, warm white. Sheer curtains let the smiling sun flow in all day.

And all the walls had color. A peachy-colored rose spread gently through the living room and halls. Blue-green bedrooms offered a place for calm, thoughtful moments. Walls were the background for paintings, full of rich, contrasting colors. Tootsie's white, orange and grey fur sparkled as she sat like Cleopatra in front of the rosy walls.

Mark sat by my special window. "That's a wonderful painting you have over there," he remarked. He pointed to a large painting at the entrance to the living room. It was a view of Tuscany seen through an open window and it was hanging on an inside wall facing into the room. At the same time it was facing a real window on the opposite wall as if trying to see outside.

He's right, I thought. My living room with its marvelous windows facing both out and in had become "a room with a view".

Self-Improvement

When Jennifer graduated Amenia High she did just what she was programmed to do. She married her childhood sweetheart, had a son, and every two years after that, she presented her hubby with another child until there were four of them, a boy and three girls.

When she turned forty-five all her children were gone and she was stunned to realize she had nothing much to do anymore. She *could* content herself cooking fish and vegetables for her husband while she ate steak and potatoes. *Not quite enough,* she thought. *That's not what I had in mind.* So she enrolled in the local community college. She thought if she could do this, she would go on to a real college, get a degree, and learn something useful—maybe even find a career.

On Monday, the first day of classes, sadly noticing a few grey hairs on her head and some more on her chin, Jennifer snuck into Composition 1.1. With any luck, no one would notice her. The hopelessly young, pretty instructor wore a short tight skirt and was weighted down with a variety of beads and imitation gold bangles. She had a small tattoo on her right hand. The teacher went to the blackboard and writing in small cramped letters, she posted the first assignment. Jennifer could barely make it out. The homework, due on Wednesday, was "Write a composition, 700 to 750 words, about Color."

Jenny's jaw dropped. A composition? By Wednesday? About color? What did she know about color? She thought about pink ribbons and blue jeans and purple tee-shirts with skeleton heads emblazoned on her son's chest, and she knew then and there that she would never make it.

Tuesday night, she sat at the kitchen table. Her hands were clammy. Her collar was too tight. She could use a drink right now—a gin and tonic—or—better yet—Johnny Walker, straight up, no rocks. She wanted to give up school, the sooner the better.

But Jenny's training had been rigorous. "Grow up! Even if you don't like something, just do it. It's good for you!"

She closed her eyes and waited for an image to draw itself on the back of her eyelids. All she saw was a rainbow. Now, this *might* be something she could write about. After all, she had brought up three daughters and each one had gone through the pink and purple and rainbow phases.

So Jenny tried to write about that. Somewhere she had heard that you should write about what you know. She knew a lot about rainbows. She had seen a lot, could draw them with crayons and Magic Markers and she could sing *all* the words to *Over the Rainbow*—by heart. She knew how to tell very vivid fairy tales but that would be disaster. She could dream up an essay on color in space. Jennifer didn't even *know* if there was color in space.

"I give up!" she exclaimed. Then with a determined "Harrumph" she hoisted herself up from the table and got her laptop. Here is what Jennifer wrote:

Dear Ms. Becker,

I have been worrying about the homework assignment since Monday and I can't imagine what you were thinking. I have pondered and ruminated and stretched my imagination to its limit.

I contemplated the stars and consulted the Oxford English Dictionary and even pored over Roget's Thesaurus, but to no avail.
This is the best that I can do.

Yours truly,
Mrs. J. White

Jennifer stuffed the letter in an envelope and on Wednesday morning she handed it in. She got an "A" for vocabulary and an "F" for content.

A Closed Door

The old woman stood in front of a closed door, afraid to open it, afraid of what she might find. The door was dark, and the hall was dark, but there was light coming from behind that door framing it as if it were a work of art. *Where's that light coming from?* she wondered. What would she find if she opened the door? Images and sounds flashed through her mind.

Maybe it was light splitting the darkness with thunder crashing behind. Maybe a lamp on a damp cellar floor. Maybe a flame, a magnet beckoning a moth to its fiery end. She heard it sizzle.

Through a wall of black she sensed something was there. *A rat,* she thought, and shrank back from those menacing red eyes. "Please," she whispered. "Please."

She stood there asking herself silent questions, exploring possible answers. Almost as if to calm herself, she began to think about light.

Light is a mystery. What is it? You can't see it when it settles on something black because black absorbs it. If it lands on something white, it bounces off—becomes invisible. It doesn't make any sense. You can't grab light, so how can it bounce off anything at all?

It was true but she couldn't understand it. *There must be more to it than just black and white. What about color? Where do we get color? All those beautiful, joyous colors—blue and gold—umber and green.*

The woman stood quietly for a long time and still could not open that door.

I hear that light is everywhere. They say it comes from the sun and it's there even at night. We just can't see it. Instead we see stars up there, looking for all the world like sparkling jewels settled against a black velvet sky. The light comes from so far away, it takes years for it to get here, so we really only see a star as it used to be.

Of course, starlight is really sunlight. She couldn't wrap her mind around that. The light was there. Could she touch it? No. Could she see it? She didn't know. Could she smell or taste it? No. But, could she feel it? Oh, yes!

Sometimes it turns the world into burning dust. Sometimes it turns the planet into a great frigid glacier. Oh yes, I can feel it!

Thoughts came rushing in so fast, words couldn't keep up. She knew that without the sun we would all die and so, she decided, it must be our friend, but if it is, it is indeed a fickle friend. A mighty, cruel master that revels in its powerful display.

In the desert the sun burns down unceasingly and you can barely breathe. Nomads try to outwit its relentless attack. They wear long caftans and wrap their heads in cloth to save their skin, and to keep themselves cool as they wander below that fiery ball.

The coldest places on Earth quake before the strength of the sun. Icicles melt. Polar bears drown in their search for food. Glaciers break apart. They calve and mountainous slices of ice fall into the warm ocean. The glaciers grow smaller and smaller and then they melt even faster. Whales appear in new places. Fishes hurry to find friendlier homes. Seals follow the fishes and sharks follow the seals.

Once, the old woman was sitting at a restaurant that overlooked a long pier. As she watched the ocean, she heard a shout from down below. A shark had come so close to land, you could see the beast chasing a lone seal. As the shark swam in figure eights, the circles grew tighter and tighter around its prey. And then there was an enormous splashing and fighting beneath the water—and the waves reaching the shore were red with the seal's blood.

"That's because of the sun too," she said out loud. But nobody answered.

In the summer the sun is so high, its light so blinding, I have to cover my eyes. And its heat is so fierce, I pray for the winter to come. In the winter, the sun is low in the sky. The slanting rays barely light the earth, the heat dissolves and the whole world shivers. I hunker down under mounds of blankets praying for the summer to come back. Then she sighed. It was too confusing.

But about one thing she was certain. When it rained and the sun was gone, the cold water beat harshly against her face. But when the sun's strength burst open those clouds, it warmed her heart so, she almost couldn't bear it.

She remembered the teacher who tried to explain the mysteries of light and color. It didn't seem important back then, but now, when her light might go out at any moment, it all seemed very important indeed.

The old woman stood in front of a closed door, afraid to open it, frightened by what she might find.

Family

Sisters Are for Loving

I love my oldest sister even though
    She thinks my jokes are ordinary
                And
    She thinks my taste in movies is ridiculous
                And
    She talks eloquently about me when it comes to women's
lib
                And
    She was embarrassed by me when I got my first divorce
                But
    She loved me even after my second divorce
                And
    She said I would get married again because I was so nice
                And
    She calls me "sweetie" when she kisses me goodnight.
My oldest sister lives in Great Barrington.

I love my younger sister even though
> She calls my poems cute
>> And
> She thinks she's just a realist instead of someone who sees the glass as ½ empty
>> And
> She sees the future through rose colored glasses when it's really going to hell in a handbasket
>> But
> She tries to cheer me up when I am really low.

My younger sister lives in New Jersey.

I loved my older sister because
> She out-witted the doctors when they said she wouldn't live to thirty-five
>> And
> She wouldn't sit down when her feet hurt
>> And
> She was too stubborn to lay down when she couldn't walk
>> And
> She was too dumb to stay in her wheelchair when they said she would never walk again,

My older sister is dead.

Grandchildren

Grandchildren are the best, they say.
They giggle, bounce
Grin like gremlins.
They try to make us laugh
And laugh out loud when we do.

Grandchildren are the best, they say.
They love us, hug us
And give us kisses.
They make us laugh and cry.
Our own sweet, soft, kittens.
They go home to spread their joy
And leave peace and quiet in their stead.

Children are the best, I say.
They are my body and my soul,
My happiest memories,
My saddest dreams.
And when they go home
They take my heart with them.

The Willow and the Oak

There is a tree in my garden that I look at every day.
I close my eyes and face them towards the sun.
I feel its warmth
See the clouds—the sky
The tree.
I look behind me
I see it still.
Then
I open my eyes.

David is here
With his strong soul
And vulnerable body.
I have held him in my arms
And he has held me up.

David is my willow tree
Cradling me in his boughs.
I am David's cloud
Watching from above
Letting the playful sunshine come through.
Together we are the smiling sun.

There is a tree in my garden that I look at every day.
The leaves grow green
Then orange—red—brown
And they fall onto the dry earth.

Daniel's beard grows from his skin
Softer and softer still
And then turns coarse.
It grows defiantly
Facing an uncaring world.

He whispers
"You must not do that.
Hold tightly.
You cannot do it alone
Or you will fall."

Daniel is my oak
Strong and stern
Urging me forward
Carefully—carefully—ever so carefully.
He teaches me to walk
Even as I weep.

Willow

Willow roared into the room—an angry lion itching for a fight. Willow—wild-haired and red-faced—screaming if anyone came near her. She demanded that we listen. She was entitled to be heard. Then she pouted, stamped her foot, and finally leaned against the wall and slid down in exhaustion.

She was quiet for a moment, then from deep within her young, small soul a new rage burst forth. "I *don't* want to be here! I'll leave! I *won't* stay another day!"

On and on it went until the nurses and the patients couldn't bear the sound any longer. We tried to escape by moving down the hall or to the Rec Room at the other end of the floor. We could still hear her. From shout to scream to hopeless wail, "Why-y-y-y-y?"

The nurses tried to reassure her. "It's going to be OK," Jessica murmured. "It's not so bad in here," Elaine cooed. They looked at each other for help but there was none.

The screaming continued and grew to a never-ending shriek. "I won't stay! I won't. You can't make me!" and the nurses told us all to go into our rooms.

A quick call on the phone. The elevator arrived, the door was unlocked, and four uniformed men stepped off. As they approached Willow, she backed against the wall. They surrounded her; they had her cornered.

"Don't touch me! I won't let you touch me!" She flailed about, arms swinging and legs kicking, but they grabbed her and held on tight, lifted her and took her to the Quiet Room.

She was still shouting as the guards left. "Can you believe it?" the tallest man sighed. "It took four men to subdue just one little girl." He shook his head as the elevator doors shut and locked behind them.

Willow was in the Quiet Room for two days. Two doors stood between that room and ours and we couldn't hear much at all. Jessica or Elaine stayed with her most of the time. When the outer door opened, we could glimpse one of them sitting in a chair by the inner doorway. Was that to keep Willow in or to keep us out?

There was a public phone in the hall where patients could get calls. When Willow got a call, she was allowed out of the room. She looked disheveled and angry. She yelled into the phone at her mother. "I need to get out of here! I have a tennis game tomorrow! I can't stay. You can't make me!" When her father called she screamed, "How could you let her put me in here? *I'm* not crazy. *She* is! Come and get me out! Now!"

Each time, she was pulled back into the Quiet Room. "I'm not going into that room again. Why do I have to?" As Willow got louder, Jessica became firmer. "If you want to come out, you have to stop shouting and behave yourself. It's your choice. You're not the only patient on the floor." The nurses were beginning to tire of the struggle.

"Spoiled brat," Dean whispered to me. "I bet nobody ever said 'no' to that kid before," Margaret added.

On the third day Willow appeared; she was clean and still. Someone had braided her hair into blonde cornrows that made her look even younger than before. For the first time I noticed she was pretty. She never spoke to anyone and never smiled, but occasionally, she seemed to drift closer to us.

There were only about a dozen patients on the floor, so each of us had space to move around with plenty of room to be alone if we wanted. Some patients paced the halls looking for something. Safety? Inner calm? Or just relief from pain? Some sat staring outward. Some were locked inside, all alone. Each did something to help find a way out. But we all had one thing in common. The need to look inside ourselves.

In the morning, we sat on benches in the dining room, a few people at each table. The ones who were ready to leave sat together joking and hoping that their release was imminent. The new ones like me, sat separately, envious of their levity. The nurses watched us and wrote down everything we ate and how much we threw away and recorded it on our charts.

Later we showered behind unlocked doors so we could be watched. Margaret never washed but walked around all day in her hospital gown. Eventually, when she began to smell, the nurses would force her into the shower room to clean her up. We made our beds, straightened up our rooms and did our private laundry.

The psychiatrist came every morning and saw each patient. A resident came with him and kept by his side so she might learn something. They would read each chart, ask the nurses about the patient's behavior and then see the patient. Every day he asked me the same thing.

"Have you ever considered killing yourself?"

"No."

"Are you sure?"

"Yes, I am."

He came closer as if to see if I was lying to him. The resident gave me a smile. "Be patient," she seemed to say.

After the doctor left, we would all sit together around a big table to see the social worker who would try to make us talk about something. This was called "group therapy". It was hopeless. Nobody said much of anything at all.

In the afternoon, we went to the Rec Room. It was a shabby looking affair. There were a few games that looked a little the worse for wear. Nobody wanted to play games. There was a lonely ping-pong table. Nobody had enough energy for that. There were pencils and crayons and some projects to weave or sew. Sewing was a problem because needles were dangerous. Someone could grab a needle, hide it and use it another time to do someone some harm. You never knew who. I was allowed to embroider outside the Rec Room since I was considered safe, non-aggressive. Of course I had to sit by the nurses' station for my own protection.

In the Rec Room, the only thing we seemed to agree on was watching movies on an old TV screen. It was like something out of "One Flew Over the Cuckoo's Nest". We stared at the screen in silence, and occasionally argued about what we wanted to see. It helped pass the boring times. If you were bored, that was a good sign. You weren't turned inward in distress or facing outward in anger.

When Willow first came to the Rec Room, we wondered why she was there. She was either judging us or she was joining us, looking for company. At first she sat apart. Then she started moving, inching her way until she sat next to me.

"I don't know why I'm here," she whispered. We sat silently for a long time. "My mother—she said she couldn't cope with me."

Silence. "My mom and dad are separated. Mom wants my kid sister, but he says 'No'. They fight about that a lot."

Willow was just a kid—not much more than thirteen or fourteen. Such a young girl without anybody she could trust. Her parents just keep fighting and screaming all the time she told me.

"I want Sherry! I want her!"

'Well, you can't take her. You don't even love her! You're just using her to get at me!'

"They never talk about me," Willow said. "I'm too much trouble." After a long pause she added, "I hope Sherry's alright. She's only ten."

The next day, Willow's dad came to visit. For the first time, she seemed happy. She ran to greet him as the elevator doors unlocked to let him in. He stepped into the ward and the doors snapped shut behind him.

She ran to hug him when he yelled, "Willow!" At last, he was here to help her. He had come to take her out. She was saved!

She chattered rapidly while her father listened stoically; he didn't say much at all.

"I'll stay out of trouble. I'll go to school, do my homework and I won't be a bother either. I'll practice tennis real hard. You'll be so proud of me!"

They went outside to the "balcony". It was a small outdoor space enclosed by bars and chicken wire to keep us from doing anything rash. There were just two places to sit and very little space to move around. Only a few people could fit at one time. Willow's father lay down on the Adirondack chair and Willow sat on the old wicker seat. She tried to talk to him.

"Tell me about your apartment. Is it big? How's Sherry? Mom promised to get her a cat. Did she get it yet?"

He smiled and closed his eyes to keep out the sun. Maybe he just didn't want to look at the bars.

"It's good," he said "—the condo I mean. There's a pool and a tennis court. You can see the golf course from my living room window. I go out and play every chance I get."

"How big is it?"

"Big enough I guess."

"Can I come and live with you? I could swim and play tennis and I'd help—make dinner—stuff like that. It'd be great!"

Her dad acted as if he hadn't heard. "You're better off with your mother."

Willow flinched and her face turned pale. They stayed there a long time. Willow didn't say much. Her father talked on and on about his job, his work—his golf scores. When he left, Willow went to her room and didn't come to dinner.

When Willow had been there five days, her mother arrived. She strode in angrily, glaring at the social worker who said her daughter could go home now. Papers were signed and the door was unlocked. The two left silently. Mother looking annoyed and weary. Daughter looking tense and depressed.

What would happen to Willow? Why had she been here anyway? We all wanted to get out from behind locked doors. We all wanted to walk about freely, sleep when we wanted, eat what we wanted, make life a bit more comfortable.

Is that what happened to Willow? We didn't really know, but we all feared she might come screaming through that door again.

I Remember

I went to the movies yesterday to see "Selma" and I wept silently in front of the big screen with its vivid images, sounds of unrelenting anger, unbearable misery and mournful prayer.

Even before I went to school, I could sing "America the Beautiful" from beginning to end and recite the "Pledge of Allegiance" bewildered by its unfathomable words. In the 4th grade I learned about the Civil War and about slavery and about Lincoln freeing the Negroes and when I looked around the room I saw a sea of white faces. In the 6th grade I learned about Jim Crow and "White's only" and "Go to the back of the bus". In high school I learned about an imaginary barrier called the Mason-Dixon Line and our capitol was south of that line and the signs said "No coloreds at this water fountain". That line was a mighty wall that even Gabriel's horn could not bring down.

When I was sixteen I went to Hootnannys and sang along with Pete Seeger and Woody Guthrie and sang "Oh Freedom" and "I'm Gonna Lay Down My Sword and Shield". In solemn unison we sang "Strange Fruit" whose words evoked images of bodies hanging from trees, bodies of innocent men tortured and lynched for crimes they did not commit.

At home I sat at the Seder table and I knew that Moses and Lincoln were brothers and in my mind I sang "Let My People Go".

I remember my father forbidding me to go to chorus practice because it was the "Interracial Chorus". I remember lying to him when I went to a midnight concert at Carnegie Hall to hear Paul Robeson sing and Willy McGee's mother plead for her son's life.

I remember bringing my black professor home to dinner one night after the class where he taught "The Negro in the United States". He looked at my father and smiled listening to my father as he lied and said he had always been fond of Negroes and he had always been very good to colored people.

I remember being an army wife in Mannheim, Germany surrounded by other soldier's wives and going to their endless coffee klatches while children were being brutally attacked by dogs and tortured with fire hoses in Arkansas because they dared to enter an all-white school. One of those army wives called me "that Nigger-lovin' Jew bastard from New York".

I remember feeling robbed when I could not march with Martin Luther King in Washington because I was "too pregnant".

I remember my son asking "Him brown?" pointing to a man at the deli counter and I tried to explain to Danny that God had made people in all colors. The man stood stiff and defiant as I spoke.

I remember Rosa Parks sitting down in the front of the bus and young people asking to be served at Woolworth's soda fountain while the Ku Klux Klan burned crosses and set fire to homes in the middle of the night.

I remember too, the moments of hope when Robert Kennedy sent federal marshals to protect the Freedom Riders and his brother sent the National Guard to defend James Meredith when he tried to register at "Ole Miss".

I remember Alabama's Governor Wallace defying LBJ. "Segregation Now, Segregation Tomorrow, Segregation Forever," he shouted but President Johnson used all his know-how and he shook hands and pressed elbows until the Voting Rights Act became law.

That was a moment in history where reason prevailed. I remember that.

Now the bravery and sacrifices of all those men and women and children resonate deep within me. And even now, their struggle for respect and rights and equality is thwarted.

So I go to the movies and I watch "Selma" and my heart aches and I weep for all the broken promises because I have watched for eighty years and my naïve childhood belief that the unfairness of it all will be changed, has been shattered beyond repair.

Revelations

In "A River Runs Through It" Norman Maclean wrote, "I am haunted by waters," a stunning end to his lyric memoir. He tells us the story of his life, full of tragedy and full of delight. His tragedy is too hard to contemplate. The death of his beautiful brother and his parents' endless silent pain. At the same time, he delights in nature, learning, family and love. His memoir is a lesson in love that transcends man's greatest trials.

I wish I could be like him. I wish I could forget about my life's small tragedies, overcome the fear of the future, and look forward to a peaceful end. Not only the end of my dreams, but the end of everyone's dreams.

I wish I could feel that sense of fulfillment other people seem to feel. I wish I could share in it. I close my eyes and search for a peaceful, quiet land. I try to see it, but I can't. I want to believe that someday there will be a place, a kind of Holy Place, where kind and caring people share Nature's bounties with all. I try to imagine it, but I can't.

I see a child running to his mother's arms, sunshine bursting forth from shining eyes. I know that overwhelming joy and my thanks rise to Heaven for that moment in Paradise. Then the child disappears and with him, so does my heart.

I see a bird. And then I see a bird of prey. I marvel at a mountain. And then mountains of mud crush the life below. I see a sunset. A storm filled cloud blots out the vision of that blazing orange sky. Even Nature fails me.

I wish I could believe in God. A God who loved us and cared for us. I wish I could reconcile that God with the one I know now, the God who watches us ruthlessly destroy each other. I try to accept it, but I can't.

Every Passover, I read from the "Haggadah", the story of the Jews' exodus from Egypt. It exhorts us to believe that what He did so long ago, He did not just for *them* but for *us*. He has brought us from slavery to freedom. My heart is filled with joy.

The story continues. "Not just one alone has risen against us to destroy us, but in every generation they rise against us to destroy us." A certain truth. We are instructed to tell this story to our children and our children's children so they will re-member God's blessing. He has led us out of Egypt. He has parted the Red Sea for us. "With a mighty hand and out-stretched arm", He freed us from our bondage and brought us to the Promised Land.

But alas, at the shore of that most wondrous place, God told Moses he could not enter. It was Aaron who led the wanderers into the Promised Land.

That phrase, "in every generation they rise against us to destroy us," has haunted me for years. Think about what it says. Think about it for just one moment. An eternity of hatred, distrust and persecution. No matter how I try I will never understand it. If it is true, and it certainly is, how can we love or trust such a God? I have seen it and the world has seen it. The truth is too harsh to acknowledge. We try to forget the horror and turn to happier times. I wish I could make that vision disappear. I try, but I can't.

There will always be some place on this Earth where obscene cruel acts are allowed, even condoned. Some people say it will get better; man created these problems so man can correct them. Some people know they are right, *they* can see it. I can't. All I see are showers, ovens, slaughter—and mountains of children's shoes.

In my mind and in my heart, there is no room for hope. There is no room for resistance or anger or even rebellion. My heart is too full of tears.

Russia-shuna

Introduction

In the fall of 2013 I was in West Hartford sitting outside enjoying a warm, sunny day. It was quiet—peaceful. No one else was around. Sitting there, I realized that it was the first day of Rosh Hashanah, the start of the Jewish New Year, the day that ushered in "The Days of Awe". It was a "High Holy Day".

I was born in 1935 in Brooklyn, surrounded by Jews who shared a common heritage. We were Shoma Shabbos, Sabbath observers who faithfully followed the laws and rituals of our ancestors who came from Eastern Europe. I was raised in an orthodox home. We kept a kosher home, went to temple regularly and were taught to respect the Old Testament and the Torah.

In 2013 I was sitting by a pool, ignoring the mandates of the day. What happened that transformed me from a religious Jew to a cultural Jew?

My sons asked me to write a memoir for them and for their children. They said it would show them how I once lived and would explain how I became what I am. I tried to think of the most memorable moments in my life. It seemed that many of them took place on Jewish holidays. Some of those memories are joyous, some are sad and still others are frightening.

I am writing my memoir about those days. For me, it is the best kind of memoir I could write. I call it "Russia-shuna" and each chapter tells the story of a Jewish holiday that I will never forget. This excerpt from the memoir includes three chapters: "Russia-shuna 1943," "Russia-shuna 1951," and "Russia-shuna 1957."

Russia-shuna 1943

The heat was oppressive, the sun was too bright, and the Jews of Brooklyn were sweating in their new fall clothes. The men wore starched white shirts and dark ties, some sported tight shoes, others wore sneakers. All the women wore hats and gloves. The ones who could afford them, flaunted their mink and fox-tail stoles. Jews got dressed up and went to pray on Russia-shuna. If the sun was shining the Christians asked "How come it's always good weather for the Jews?" If it rained they were exultant. "They really got it this time. Chosen people? Ha!"

When I was a kid back in 1943, we said "Russia-shuna" and "Yum-kipper" with the syllables all mashed together to make a clip-clop sound. A horse trotting along—Russia-shuna, Yum-Kipper—Russia-shuna, Yum-Kipper. We said it with the Yiddish inflection that had a certain flair—a unique kind of panache. Nowadays, we carefully say "Rosh Hashanah" and "Yom Kippur" in Hebrew. It loses something in Hebrew I think. The rhythm is gone. There's no more music, no more magic.

Jews use Yiddish with its endless supply of idioms. There are reams of them with phrases that create outrageous images in the mind. They reveal our weaknesses and deflate our over-weaning egos. We joke and tease and in that way, we can see ourselves and our foibles for what they really are. But the jokes are ours. God forbid anyone else should use them.

Sometimes, Yiddish idioms are answers to foolish questions. If I ask "Where is the frying pan?" I get the answer "Twenty years in the Rabbi's house and you still don't know that the cat has no tail?"

Yiddish commands are very colorful. "Chop me no teakettles" for "Go away, don't bother me".

And sometimes they are weird curses. "You should grow like an onion with your head in the ground and your feet in the air."

Yiddish is the lingua franca of Eastern European Jews. A Hungarian Jew meeting a Rumanian Jew finds a comfortable connection. They are *landsmen,* people from the same land.

In Poland and Russia and all those other countries east of Germany, orthodox Jews revered Hebrew and held it sacred. It was the language of the Old Testament, the Torah, the Law. At home, they spoke Ashkenazi Yiddish, the one we call Yiddish today. In Western Europe, assimilated Jews, avoided that language. Today, many people avoid it because it sounds "too German".

My parents were first generation Americans and we spoke English in my home. Yiddish was the adult language saved for secrets and intimate words. It was used to shield the children. There was time enough for them to hear about the ugly present and the ominous future.

When Israel was created in 1948 a decision had to be made. What should be the official Israeli language, one that both native born Sabras and immigrant displaced persons would use? Yiddish, despite its many dialects, could bring them all together. Hebrew, as a secular language, would have to be learned.

In fact, Hebrew was the most practical choice—the only one that would work. Yiddish was the language of Eastern Europe. Most Ashkenazi Jews had been swallowed up in the jaws of the German machinery. After the Holocaust most of them were gone. Their culture and language were destroyed in bonfires fed by murderous, stupid little men.

People say that Yiddish is a dying language but it stubbornly hangs on. If it ever disappears it will be a tragedy. Not only is it the glue that holds us together, it is too beautiful to lose.

Russia-shuna in 1943 is still clear in my mind. Here is the world as seen through a child's eye.

My sister Barbara was the oldest of the "Four Mintz Girls" and she was beautiful. She seemed *much* older to me but she was only fourteen. I thought she was stunning.

"Barbara should be in the movies! Someone from Hollywood should come to Brooklyn and give her a screen test. She would be a star!"

Rachel, the second of our quartet, was eleven. She was the most cheerful and outgoing of us all. With her happy, smiling face, she too was a beauty. She was comfortable no matter where she was and she grew up to be Perle Mesta wherever she went. She always greeted you with her open, warm smile that put you at ease, any place, any time and under any circumstances.

I was the number three Mintz girl. I was eight years old. I don't remember how I looked but it really didn't matter. I felt dumb and stupid and insignificant compared to Barbara and Rachel. I was especially miserable at *Shul*, especially on the Jewish holidays. The Congregation Ahaveth Israel on Avenue K was so big and grey and ugly—and I was bored to death. I wanted to go home.

The youngest sister was Ronnie, Ronnie Sue to be exact, a moniker given to her by Barbara who wasn't at all fond of old fashioned Biblical names. My mother thought, that if Barbara got to choose the name, maybe she wouldn't mind another baby in the family. You see, Barbara thought it was a shame to see my mother walking around with a big belly. My mother had done it just to embarrass her.

It was forbidden to ride on the holidays so we had to walk to temple. Sometimes, when it was too far or too hot to walk, the "heathens" drove over and parked their cars far enough away where they hoped no one would see. Ronnie couldn't get a ride because we couldn't push the carriage. Since there was no way she could walk that long half mile each way to *Shul* and back again, she stayed home. If she *had* been there, I could just hear everyone ooh-ing and aah-ing and saying "look at that smile" and "isn't she adorable?" So I hated her!

Now, there's a different way to describe the structure of this four-girl sorority.

Barbara was the chief, the one left in charge when my mother went out. Barbara was the Master Sergeant who kept the troops in line until the Inspector General came home. The job was an honor—a tribute to her intelligence, loyalty and good judgment. She was the oldest and smartest, so there you had it. She took the job seriously and exerted her temporary power sternly. "What would mother say if I told her that?" We answered back and taunted her and grumbled but she was after all, "the one who must be obeyed".

Rachel followed in Barbara's footsteps and never could quite live up to the high standards set by her older sibling. Mean-spirited teachers in P.S. 152 asked Rachel, "Are you as smart as your big sister?" When I started school, it became an insidious competition. "Who's the smartest one?" By the time they saw Ronnie sitting at the spot that had "Mintz" worn into the seat, they were amazed and tired. "What? *Another* Mintz girl?" They exchanged knowing glances, raised their eyebrows, all the while mumbling something about rabbits.

Once, I was the youngest, pampered baby but my position was usurped when Ronnie was born. True, I was no longer at the bottom of the pecking order, but now, with her arrival, I was demoted to just a middle child. Humiliating! I could sense right away that I was a misfit destined to become the family rebel, the black sheep, the skeleton in the closet.

Ronnie obeyed Barbara and Rachel and was in awe of them. With me, it was a different story. I was almost seven years her senior, but she never listened to me at all. As soon as she could talk, it became my duty to "keep an eye" on her when my mother was busy. With a conventional husband, four children, and a few indigent relatives, how could she *not* be busy? I had to take Ronnie with me when I played with my friends. An albatross around my neck who hung there contributing nothing. She was a royal pain in the ass. My friends wouldn't let me play if "the baby" was around.

"Go away! Leave us alone. I can't stand you!" I shouted.

"I can so play! You have to let me! Mommy sssshed!" she would respond defiantly. Ronnie spoke with a sloppy wet lisp as she squeezed the "S" out through the sides of her mouth.

Our relationship could jump from hot to cold in minutes. We fought a lot. But once in a blue moon, I felt protective of her and we stuck close together. It's a blessing that she doesn't remember my temper. Perhaps that's her way of saying "It doesn't really matter anymore."

The Mintzes were strictly *Shoma Shabbos*. We observed all the rules and dictates of the Sabbath and Jewish holy days. Sometimes we all went to Friday night services. Sometimes my father went without us. But on Russia-shuna there was no choice. We all *had* to go to *Shul*. My parent expected it and there would be the usual hell to pay if we didn't come.

The three of us didn't have to be at temple too early. We were girls and nobody really expected us to pray. So by the time we got there, all the grownups were inside praying and the girls were outside showing off their new fall outfits and flirting with the boys.

I was too young to flirt and didn't actually know how. There certainly wasn't anybody there that I'd choose to show me. Instead, I tried to attract one of Barbara's friends, Gene. He used to come over to our house which was the place where the Midwood High School gang would hang out after school. They laughed a lot and drank gallons of Pepsi Cola and marveled over mom's blintzes. And Gene always took some time to talk to me and tell me how beautiful I was getting.

I needed a partner so I crept up to the group and stood there. Gene noticed me and gave out a big whooping yell and all the guys smiled and said "Hello". Okay, that wasn't too bad. In fact, it was amazingly easy. I could do this. When I turned away the guys all laughed and Gene said I was cute. *Cute? Cute is for puppies. Cute is for kittens. Cute is not for me!*"

Some kids wandered in and out of Shul. The Mintz girls did not. We stayed outside until suddenly the air became electric and the three of us turned toward the synagogue entrance. As if it were timed, my father sauntered out with a friend, ostensibly to catch a breath of air. He pulled a freshly ironed handkerchief from his breast pocket, mopped his brow and nonchalantly looked around.

The three of us stood at attention, as tall as we possibly could. I stood on tip-toe. Would he see me and my overbearing sisters? He might not notice us at all—but he always did. The Major examined his troops, puffed up his chest, nudged the man next to him and nodded in our direction. He looked around and smiled modestly as if to say "you think *your* troops are good? Look at *mine!*"

We intuited his order, "Okay soldiers—at ease!" He turned smartly and went back to pray.

Sometimes we stayed to hear the cantor "blow the Shofar". The Shofar is the ram's horn Jews use to call to each other. It looks a bit like a cornucopia gone awry, a small inauspicious instrument. A child's toy—extremely difficult to play. It produces two distinctive sounds—the first low and deep, the second high and sharp. It calls out "d'DAH dit—d'DAH dit," a strong defiant sound ending with an abrupt upward flourish. The sound must be played in perfect cadence and the exact pitch to be heard by every Jew. For centuries it has summoned Jews to come together to pray or to defend themselves, the two most important things in Jewish history.

It has become the symbol of unity and strength to our community.

The older kids giggled, and rolled their eyes "Blow the chauffer! Blow the chauffer!" I didn't get the joke.

There's a story about the call to rumble in Leonard Bernstein's "West Side Story". Originally, Bernstein planned to write his musical drama about Jews fighting for their place in New York. Instead it was the fight between the American Jets and the not-so-American Sharks, gangs that ruled the Upper West Side. In a stroke of genius, Bernstein used that Shofar music to call the warring gangs to fight. "d'DAH dit—d'DAH dit." It rang out eerie, militant and mournful. No one will ever forget that sound echoing from the stage in a darkened theater or from the screen in a crowded movie house.

Occasionally my father invited us to come in and sit on the women's side of the aisle. I watched the men sway back and forth, back and forth. Each man read the Hebrew prayers softly but the combined voices became a chorus sent upward to the ear of God himself.

When it was time to blow the Shofar, young and old crowded into the temple. We stood in the back because we didn't have seats. Even though we couldn't see the horn, its commanding, mournful sound rang through the synagogue crying into each listening ear. Even now, when I go to temple, the cry of the Shofar reminds me of the rare times when my father and I were happy together. And at the same time, I'm reminded of the anger we often shared.

After we had officially arrived at *Shul*, and my father stopped *kvelling* we rushed home to set the table for the holiday lunch. My mother always managed to get everything ready before she left for services. The cooking was done and the kitchen was clean. She put on her best clothes with a hat and gloves. She never had the furs to wear but she always had a new hat. She would take me on her annual trip to the milliners. While I tried on broad brimmed hats decorated with feathers and birds, she went for the small black ones with modest veils.

That was the typical holiday scenario. But once, years later, my father walked out of a Russia-shuna service. The annual appeal was in progress. The president of the congregation got up and asked for donations to the mortgage fund, or the fund to refurbish the leaky roof or whatever else the congregation needed.

It was standard procedure to include the appeal at the start of the Jewish New Year. Everyone was there, even the once-a-year crowd. Between the practice of charging people for their seats, and the money raised at the appeal, the temple would meet its budget. All year long, in any Shul, no one passed a plate. There was no tithing. On the High Holy Days, the "now-and-then crowd" showed up and the practice took hold.

At a break in the mid-morning service, the women left and the men stayed behind. The president of the congregation rose and the appeal began.

"Mr. Cohen gave us $500 this year. Thank you, Mr. Cohen, we can always count on you. So what about you, Mr. Schwartz, you had a good year too. How much are you going to pledge? And Mr. Mintz, how about you?"

My father rose and went outside. "How could they embarrass people that way? To call out names in public?" my father asked. The answer? "That's just the way things are done."

Later that year, he resigned from his position as Vice President of Congregation Ahaveth Israel.

Howard Mintz was once a rich man, but the Great Depression had left him poor. He rarely spoke about it, but when he did you heard the voice of a man ashamed of his plight. He did not want the world to know.

Like farmhands at the ring of a bell, my whole family always sat down to supper at the same time. There were my parents, the girls, and at least one aunt. For a while, there was my brother-in-law too. Even before Mark and Barbara were engaged, he came for supper and that was a great day for my father. There was another male at the table! Mark got up to carry his dirty plate to the kitchen and dad roared, "No! No man in my house helps with the housework!" Surprised, visibly delighted, Mark sat down. I fumed.

There were so many of us, we ate supper in the dining room at the big mahogany table. It was long and heavy with big, round carved legs you could rest your feet on and kick with your shoes. As soon as my legs were long enough, I learned that kicking the table felt good and sounded better. But there would be no noise at that table. It had to be perfectly silent while the voice on the radio brought us the news from the war in Europe. Every night we listened to grim reports about the war in Germany with hints about the plight of European Jews. It frightened the adults and terrified the kids. Supper was a somber affair.

Not so on Russia-shuna. Before our parents came home for lunch, we set the table in grand fashion. The beautiful linen tablecloth and napkins were spread. The polished silverware stood at attention alongside our best gilt-edged china.

The wine and water glasses sparkled. A bottle of sweet red wine was ready in front of my father's seat. And in the center of the table, we lovingly placed the special Rosh Hashanah round challah. The smell of chopped liver, chicken soup and pot roast permeated the air. Apple slices were ready to dip into honey so we might savor the sweetness the New Year would bring.

My father poured the wine and we all thanked the Lord for giving us "the Fruit of the Vine." Even the youngest got a taste. The challah was cut and we thanked the Lord for giving us "the Bread from the Earth." We broke off pieces of that warm, sweet bread, tasted it, and, with a smile, sat down to this century old feast.

Rosh Hashanah ushers in the "Days of Awe". We pray to God and he will decide our fate for the coming year. It is the time when we ask those we have wronged to forgive us for any wrongdoing we have done them. Without that for-giveness, God will not grant us forgiveness. Young as I was, it made me feel good. I thought things would get better. No more war, no more being afraid.

I think Rosh Hashanah means the same to me now. I still continue to wait for the good times even though I believe they will never come. Perhaps that is why I sit alone on Russia-shuna nostalgic for things that never were.

Russia-shuna 1951

Once again it was a hot day, but in 1951 it was Erev Russia-shuna and the setting sun would usher in the start of the "Days of Awe". In 1951 the air was electric with anticipated joy. The Brooklyn Bums were playing the New York Giants for the National League pennant.

Now you should know, that in 1951 the Brooklyn Dodgers meant as much to our borough as the appearance of the three kings meant to Christianity. We followed our team's every moment of every game of every season.

On summery Saturday nights, all my aunts, uncles and cousins would meet at Aunt Lena's house for cake and coffee and a glass of Schnapps. The kids played outside until it was too dark to see. The grown-ups stayed inside, eating, and sipping steaming tea through lumps of hard sugar held between their teeth. They talked heatedly about the latest game. They argued about scores and batting averages until my Aunt Ella would interrupt. "What Peewee Reese did—it's good for the Jews?"

Going into the end of the season that year, the Dodgers were way ahead. Everyone knew they were a shoo-in. If they

won the pennant, there was a slim chance—a quiet hope—
that at last they would face and defeat the hated, invincible
Yankees—those "Damn Yankees". Just a few weeks later, the
Giants had caught up with our home boys. We couldn't believe it. It was beyond comprehension! There had to be a three
game playoff!

The first game went to the Giants on their home turf and
we began to sweat. The second one went to the Dodgers at
Ebbets Field and we began to hope. But we began to worry
too. We petitioned whoever, to postpone the next night's
game at the Polo Grounds until after Russia-shuna to give us a
chance to pray. And—incidentally, it would give our team a
non-holy day of rest.

No luck. The crucial deciding game must go on. I don't
think there were any Jews on the two teams, but that would
have made no difference. In 2015 it's different. The Jews have
Moe Berg, Hank Greenberg and Sandy Koufax, just to mention a few baseball greats to brag about.

On Erev Russia-shuna, we had to eat a very fast dinner so
we would be in temple by sundown. What a rush. The news
spread like wildfire throughout the neighborhood. The game
was still in progress but we had to leave.

As we rushed down the street, passing by each house, we
could hear radios blaring. The game followed us and we followed the game.

Back in the Bronx, it was the bottom of the ninth with
two outs and the Dodgers were ahead by two runs. The Giants had three men on base. The Bums brought in Ralph
Branca, their best lead-off pitcher. Just one more strike-out or
one more pop-up to Center Field—one more line drive to the
outfield—and we would triumph. As we hurried along our

hearts kept pace with our feet. And then—we heard the crack of a bat.

Andy Pafko raced back—back—back—to the left field wall, reached high up for the dropping sphere—and the ball sailed over that wall and kept on going. Bobby Thompson hit a grand-slam home run called "the shot heard 'round the world!"

A great hurrah came from the Giant fans in the stands. A soft moan came from the Dodger fans at the game. A quiet wail rose to the heavens from the Jews of Brooklyn as Rosh Hashanah, once more, began with a mournful, pleading wail.

Russia-shuna 1957

In May of 1957 I went to Mannheim, Germany to be with my husband. Bob was a PFC assigned to an infantry division, part of the NATO forces stationed in West Germany. We were newly-weds, living "on the economy". In other words we had to live off-base using the small stipend that was supposed to pay for our own housing. All army wives got a monthly allotment check and that helped buy food and assorted sundries. There was a Commissary to buy American food products and the PX where you could find anything else you needed. Without them, we could not get by.

Soldiers were subject to German law and had to follow all military rules and regulations as well. I was a dependent. By some strange logic, I was part of the army and there were military rules governing me. I had an American passport but I belonged to the army anyway. I didn't wear a uniform but shorts and slacks were absolutely forbidden. At all times I had to be a shining example of American good taste and respect. If I didn't obey all the rules, I would be sent home.

It's wrong to make generalizations. I know that, but I couldn't help noticing that these rules were strictly enforced for "enlisted men". Officers and their families would stride through Europe demanding better toilet paper and ordering steak and French fries in the finest gourmet restaurants available. They were the only ones with enough money to throw around and they threw their weight around as well. They were loud, rowdy drunks totally obnoxious earning us the title "Ugly Americans".

We found an apartment house on the Ringstrasse, the street that formed a ring around inner Mannheim. The building was owned by Herr Rothermühl and his stolid wife. I couldn't read the lease but I knew what it said. We both had to sign it. Bob went first. When he came to the blank line labeled *Frommigeitt* he looked at me. Perhaps I knew that word. I nodded and we both wrote "Jewish". Herr Rothermühl raised his eyebrows, smiled knowingly and queried "Ah, Juden?" Frau Rothermühl frowned. I froze. It was an omen of things to come.

Our landlords owned an appliance store on the ground floor. The building had three upper floors with four furnished apartments on each. On each floor there were two toilets in the hall to be shared by all four apartments. Each unit contained one large room with a miniscule kitchen. Two people couldn't stand in it at the same time. There was a two burner stove and a small oven. A few cabinets held the scant supply of dishes and glasses.

The kitchen served as a shower room as well. There was a small square curtained shower in the left hand corner. To the right of the shower stood a clean shiny hand basin. The Germans were nothing if not clean. There was not an inch to spare on the whole wall.

When I wanted a shower, I pulled the curtain around me and it formed a wet, clinging cocoon of privacy. I closed my eyes and pretended there was a toilet nearby so I had the illusion, at least, that I was in a real bathroom.

I went to the PX and bought an American dish rack and stood it on the shower floor. The room was transformed into a kitchen. I washed the dishes in the hand basin, I put them in the rack to drain and made believe that there was a sink nearby and a kitchen table to boot.

Our living-dining-bedroom was filled with a large bed, one easy chair and a very small table with two wooden chairs. There was a hanging crystal lamp with three 40-watt bulbs. There were no closets but a huge *Schrank* we stuffed with everything we owned. Spoiled Americans that we were, we bought a new tiny refrigerator, on time of course, one that the Rothermühls hoped to re-possess when we left. They had a sense that Americans never would pay off the entire debt. Then they would sell it to a new, spoiled, military replacement.

The place was almost fully occupied by U.S. Army personnel who expected heat and hot water. There was an Indian engineer on our floor as well and he was there on an expense account from Daimler-Benz. The Rothermühls could charge anything they wanted.

Bob would report to the base every morning and I would stare out the window onto the street below. I could see the buildings across the street and the railroad station, the *Bahnhof,* on the right. Every city and decent sized town in Germany had a *Bahnhof* in its center which opened onto the main thoroughfare. I could see people meeting and shaking hands. Even women and children had mastered the art of a strong handshake. I watched women walking arm in arm down the street while their well-mannered children followed closely behind. I heard the squeal of tires when a motorcyclist lost control. And I heard that blood-chilling shriek of an ambulance as it rushed to help. The sounds remained from the war days when that terrible two-note alarm heralded the arrival of the SS.

Bob was the only college graduate in his platoon who had any skills other than handling rifles and spit shining shoes. A lot of the men on base didn't have any smarts. They were eligible for dum-dum discharges which they refused. They were enlisted men during the time of Universal Military Training when a two year tour of duty was required for every able-bodied young man. They chose to "re-up" to become career soldiers and retire on full army pay after twenty years of service. Not bad for men who could barely read and write.

"Is there anyone here who can type?"

Bob, saluting, "I can! Sir!"

"OK soldier, report to this office tomorrow at oh-seven-hundred hours. Dis-missed!"

Not only was Bob the only college graduate on post, he was the only Jew.

"Hey, I never met a fuckin' Jew before. Where's ya' horns?"

"You stupid or somethin'? Ain't you seen them fuckin' caps they wear and their fuckin' curlicues? There ain't no fuckin' space to hide no fuckin' horns!"

"I seen Jews before. Hey, Wilensky! How come you don't wear fur hats with them black shiny coats with the strings hangin' down?"

"I'm a Jew. We're the same as anyone."

"Sez who, you fuckin' Christ killer!"

I can't understand why Americans are so smug, act so superior and treat other countries and cultures with such disdain. We travel around the world admiring ourselves, thinking the United States is an example of Democracy, where all people are equal and have a chance to make something of themselves because Americans are fair and ready to share their bounty. But we won't admit to ourselves that we treat our own countrymen as if they were not like us. As if they were a threat to us when they tried to move out of their allotted space.

For the most part, these apartments on the Ringstrasse were home to American army couples. The husbands left every day to work at the "post" and returned every evening for supper. The wives cleaned and cooked and baked mounds of chocolate chip cookies. They went to the commissary for food and the PX for everything else. They shopped there because they were non-profit, duty-free stores, but also because the women couldn't speak a word of German. They couldn't find *wasser* in their German-English dictionaries because it didn't begin with a "V".

Mid-morning there was the ladies' coffee break. They would sit around and gossip about the ones who hadn't shown up that day. They would swap recipes and talk about going back home to a real country where they could have babies and raise them the right way. I was invited now and then. I wasn't a regular.

While I was in Mannheim, trying to befriend both Germans and Americans, a disaster was raging in Little Rock. It was something I felt ashamed about. My army wife neighbors thought it was disgusting too, but in a different way. They were furious that niggers were fighting for something they didn't deserve.

When Bob went out on maneuvers for ten days there was a party in the building and everyone was invited. Everyone except me, that is. I was lonely and miserable and could hear laughing and loud music coming from the apartment below. In typical army wife fashion, I baked some chocolate chip cookies and crashed the party. The women were outraged, their embarrassed husbands extended a cool welcome. I was handed a drink and sat down. Then Angela, a college graduate and high school teacher from Detroit, pointed at me and proclaimed, "See her? You can't trust her. She's a nigger-lovin' Jew bastard from New York!"

Some of the revelers were dumbstruck. Most of them laughed. To this very day, it was to me, the most hurtful thing that anyone had every said out loud. It was said proudly, a degrading and insulting challenge. But, of course, I am one of the lucky ones.

When September came around, Bob decided we should go to *Shul* for Rosh Hashanah services. He went to Major Clark and asked for two days special leave to observe the High Holy Days that began on sundown of the first night and lasted until sunset two days later.

The Major had never heard of Rosh Hashanah. He had no idea why it took so many days and couldn't believe it would start in mid-week at sundown. Any special leave was in addition to normal leave which meant that the annual leave of 30 days was extended to 32. Major Clark would never encourage that.

Bob explained that it was the Jewish New Year that ushered in the "Days of Awe". Jews prayed in temple for forgiveness for their sins and for health in the coming year. The Major thought a bit then said there was a chaplin on base and he could probably run the service.

"With all due respect, Sir, there are Hebrew prayers and psalms and the B'rucha over the challah and Kosher wine. Sir!"

"I'm sure we can get those things in the Chapel by next week, soldier."

"But sir, Jews are not allowed to work on the Sabbath and the Jewish Holidays. And we're not allowed to drive. We have to walk everywhere. Sir!"

The base was a few miles outside of Mannheim.

"I'll think about it soldier, and tell you tomorrow. Dismissed!"

Suddenly, the only Jew in town, became a person to be envied. The G.I.s couldn't believe that being Jewish would get you two days extra leave. It was just another one of those tricks that kikes were so good at.

On Tuesday, Bob polished his shoes, put on his uniform and went out to find the only synagogue in Mannheim. It was just a few streets away and he thought it might be better if he went alone. In full army dress uniform, a half hour before sundown, he left.

He came home a few hours later. It wasn't too far away after all, he just had some trouble finding it. The service was good and the people were friendly and we would both go in the morning.

The next day, I put on my dark blue suit, modest blue hat, low heeled pumps, and left my pocketbook at home in deference to the real Sabbath observers. Bob put on his uniform and we left.

As we walked through Mannheim people avoided us for no other reason than an American uniform was avoided. Germans were wary of us and resented us for having once leveled their city. They chose not to think about how America had rebuilt Germany before any other nation had recovered from the war. The U.S. would use it as a bulwark against the Russians in the east. And even though Germany wanted that protection, we were unwelcome guests.

Bob and I walked down some tree-lined streets that led up to an open space. There was a large lawn and a low-slung building in the center. There were no markings on the walls. It looked like a community center. Bob took my arm and led me into the building.

We entered the lobby. There was not a soul in sight. In front of us we saw a pair of doors. Bob opened the door and gently escorted me in like a very special visitor. I saw the Holy Ark and the Torah. I saw a large room with pews with space for two hundred people. I saw a handful of people sitting in the first few rows. This was all that remained of the Jews in Mannheim. More than 12,000 Mannheim Jews had been deported and sent to the death camps. There were less than one hundred families left.

Twenty heads turned to look at us. Twenty pairs of eyes filled with fear and turned away. Some men nodded at Bob and greeted him joyfully. It was good to have a new member, even if it was only for a few days. As for me, the men stared at me coldly. The women sent furtive glances my way.

Bob moved to the left row of pews. I sat behind the women on the right. I took a prayer book from the rack in front of me. It was in Hebrew and German. Bob opened his book. It was in Hebrew and English.

The service continued. Bob smiled as he followed the service as best he could. I sat bowed over my book hoping to match up the Hebrew I heard with the Hebrew I could once read. Then the congregation began to sing the call to the people of Israel.

> *Sh'ma Yis-ro-eil:*
> *A-do-nai E-lo-hei-nu:*
> *A-do-nai E-chad!*

> *Hear, O Israel:*
> *The Lord is our God,*
> *The Lord is One!*

And then I began to cry. I cried for my father who had taught me this prayer. I cried for my mother who had shown me the comfort of this place. And I cried for the people of Mannheim who were gone. *What have they done to my people? How could God have let it happen?*

When the service was over, the women gathered round and we spoke to each other. They spoke in their German and Yiddish. I spoke in my broken German and broken Ashkenazi Yiddish. We said the prayer over the warm sweet wine.

> *B'ruch atah, A-donai*
> *E-lo-hei-nu, Me-lech Ho-a-lam*
> *Bo-rei p'ri ha-ga-fun.*

Blessed art Thou our God
King of the Universe,
Creator of the fruit of the vine.

We said the prayer over the sweet round challah.

B'ruch atah, A-donai
E-lo-hei-nu, Me-lech Ho-a-lam
Bo-rei p'ri ho-a-do-mah.

Blessed art Thou our God
King of the Universe,
Who has brought forth the bread from the earth.

Bob and I walked home in silence. What kind of tribute could we pay to the millions who had been slaughtered by our German neigbors? How could we keep silent and forgive such atrocities?

When we got home I cried again. We didn't go to temple the next day. We stayed home, said the *Sh'ma* and the *B'rucha* and drank the sweet wine. Then we cut the sweet round challah. The sweetness was for the hope of a sweet year to come. I was taught that the challah was round because we wished our lives to be safe, without sorrow at its edges.

But that will never happen. Our cries rise up to a distant, uncaring God.

A Foot in the Door

Introduction

In 1952 if you said "computer", people thought you were talking about a newfangled adding machine. In 1953 a few people called computers "electronic brains". By the time I was hired as a programmer trainee in 1956, the word programming was around but no one knew what it was.

I was lucky to fall into a job in a challenging new industry. I retired in January of this year after 60 years of active participation in that industry. I worked on the UNIVAC I, the first commercially sold computer—ever. I lived through the era of IBM supremacy, witnessed the rise of PCs accompanied by the ever-changing role of professional and not-so-professional software designers.

In the '50s no one knew what the computer world would be. It was a new field with few rules. Women could get a foot in the door before it became part of the "old boy's network". From the exalted age of 80, I look back and try to see how we got from there to here.

This excerpt "A Foot in the Door" is the opening section of a memoir I call "In at the Beginning or How I Went from Pioneer to Dinosaur in 60 Short Years". It describes how this young woman managed to enter that new and exciting industry.

In the Pool

"Where are you going?"

"Princeton."

"That was my first choice too. They turned me down. I'm going to Cornell."

"Sorry."

"What's to be sorry about? They have girls in Cornell!"

"Did you hear that Eric got a full scholarship to MIT? Books, room and board—the works."

"No surprise. He was 15th ranking student."

"Yeah." Thoughtful pause. "I guess. But even so, he's lucky. I wouldn't mind a full scholarship. Even just $250 a year. Any kind of scholarship. Boy, what I could do with that much cash!"

"Hey, Martha. Where are you going?"

"Brooklyn College."

I walked away.

When I graduated Summa Cum Laude from Midwood High School, 10th in a class of 581 students, I was facing a bleak future. It wasn't right. Where was justice? I *had* the grades and I *needed* the money.

I knew I could get a scholarship but I needed my parents' approval to apply. My father refused to sign anything. He simply would not sign something where he had to tell someone how much he had. Not so, I tried to explain. Scholarships were given on merit not need. He stood fast, so I stayed in Brooklyn.

To rise above adolescent angst and puppy love into the world of maturity and great wisdom was the start of a great journey. Colleges and universities were nestled at the foot of mountains, in peaceful countrysides, alongside cool streams that fed great rivers that travelled out to sea. Brooklyn College was sitting in the heart of Flatbush on Bedford Avenue, one block over from Midwood High. Entering college was a rite of passage, a crossing from childhood to adult. To make that crossing, all I had to do was cross at the corner by the traffic light.

My future, to say the least, was unappealing. To be honest, I couldn't image what my future would be at all. All I knew was I was broke and I needed a job that summer. I didn't want to work as a waitress, or a full-time babysitter and being a nurses' aide was the pits.

I was a high school honor student, damn it! I was made for better things. I would work in a lovely air-conditioned office overlooking Central Park with plants on the windowsill and Musak in the air. I would sit at an oak desk answering the phone, typing letters and filing papers in perfect alphabetical order. People would smile at me as they passed, admiring the young, enchanting, college-bound young woman.

Unfortunately, my office skills had a lot to be desired. In fact, I had never worked in an office in my life. All I knew about offices I picked up from watching movies where blond beauties snared unsuspecting bosses and, at the end, they walked hand in hand into the sunset. I could type some, but I was self-taught and never did conquer the art of using the top row of numbers and special character keys.

Diligently, every day, I pored over the Help Wanted section of the New York Times and finally found an ad. "Typist wanted, no experience necessary." Just what I needed so I applied for the job at the Barrett Division of the Allied Chemical & Dye Corporation on Rector Street in downtown Manhattan.

First I met a lady in Personnel. We talked about my school, my grades and any part time jobs I ever had. She wanted to know why someone with my grades and experience, even as little as it was, wanted to work as a clerk typist. I mumbled something evasive and passed Interview Part 1.

Next, I went to see an old-ish looking woman with grey hair and laced up shoes. She was going to give me a typing test. It didn't matter how fast I typed, she said, speed would come with practice. Accuracy was mandatory. She handed me a sample letter. It was three paragraphs long to be typed in true business letter style. There was a date, name and address, salutation and the final "Yours Truly".

It was an important moment. I sat down at an antique Underwood manual typewriter, looked around at the grey walls, grit my teeth and ever so slowly, as if I were taking the College Boards, I did it. She looked it over very carefully and told me I had passed. It was true that I had not left enough space between the date line and the addressee—but I would learn that in time.

I landed the job but there was just one problem. I was looking for a summer job and this job was permanent. I was asked to promise that I would not quit in the fall to go to college. *I might go to Hell for this, but I need this job.* So I smiled shyly and lied through my teeth. I said I had worked part time at the Avenue J branch of the Brooklyn Public Library for fifty cents an hour and I needed more than that. Smiling, nodding and silently praying, I landed the worst job in the world. A typist in a "Typing Pool".

The only difference between a typing pool and a swimming pool is that the first is filled with water and women sit by it drinking cool lemonade, and the second is filled with sweat and women sit there hunkered down over grey manual typewriters.

There were probably hundreds of typing pools in New York. It wasn't really all that bad. But being in a typing pool had no class. If, on the other hand, you were a stenographer, a job in the Steno Pool had no class either, but it paid better.

I looked at my future colleagues. There were a few young girls with no interest whatsoever in going to school. Each one was patiently waiting to meet a good looking guy to marry. He would give her a lovely house with a real pool where she would play bridge, drink lemonade and live happily ever after. The majority of the women in the place were sluggish and single. They had waited around but they were never rescued and eventually became resigned to their fate. Finally, there were old ladies with curved backs and necks they had grown after a lifetime of leaning over typewriters—putting accuracy before speed, of course. The golden age group worked quietly and sighed because they needed the money or why else would they be here.

There was not a man in sight.

The first Monday in July, there was orientation for all the new clerks. There were four of us. We eyed each other suspiciously, worrying which one of us would increase her speed first. Maybe BDAC&DC didn't really need all four of us. But there was something else we could sense about each other. We were all partners in crime. We had broken the 9th commandment lying about our plans and we had broken the 10th commandment by coveting other people's cash.

The supervisor of the typing pool was Miss Sullivan. She was a dedicated Barrett Division employee. She had given them the best years of her life and you could tell. By the end of the day, we had dubbed her "Miss S" or "Boss Lady".

Boss Lady smiled and told us to make ourselves comfortable. She told us, if we tried very hard and stayed at our typing stations and minded our own business, we could learn enough to rise up from the pool. I looked around at the metal typing tables and armless typing chairs. The only sound was the tap tap tap of the typewriter keys. *Lazarus rising from the grave,* I thought.

Each of the four of us, Miss S continued, could be promoted upstairs to work for a Sales Manager. Upstairs each manager had a private cubicle. Clerk typists sat outside the cubicles. There, we would use our advanced typing skills and learn some new office procedures as well—how to answer phones, take messages, and make a good cup of coffee.

All the salesmen were men. All the clerks were women.

How to describe the pool itself? It was an enormous warehouse suitable for storing supplies and discarded machinery. The décor was turn of the century New York, Early Sweat Shop. Endless rows of clerks sat at typing tables and their chairs faced east. Miss Sullivan sat in a private cubby with a desk and a chair and a filing cabinet. She faced west and looked through a large glass window which allowed her to monitor her staff. She was ever vigilant in her search for someone out of line.

The building itself was *not* air-conditioned. We had to make do with open windows and fans. Status was measured by an employee's distance from a window. Every promotion meant a better location. As typists moved up in the ranks they moved nearer and nearer to the windows. The newcomers were in the seats next to the bathroom.

The room was grey, the floors were grey and every day was grey. We sat at our desks and did what we were told.

The Rule: You can leave your desk for a forty-five minute lunch break. In addition, once in the morning and once in the afternoon, you can take a five minute break to go to the Ladies' Room. The break was to be used only if nature called or if you wanted a smoke.

At 10:30 a.m. on my first day of work, I went to the Ladies' for my five minute break. Miss Sullivan followed me to see what I was up to. Pee, poop or Pall Mall. I was simply stretching my neck and back. This was insubordination and had to be nipped in the bud. Boss Lady repeated the rule. I was not entitled to a rest break, only a cigarette break. At lunch time I bought a pack of Philip Morris cigarettes thereby beginning a long addiction to those deadly pacifiers.

At 5:00 p.m., all hot and sweaty, everyone ran to the elevators. The room fell silent behind us. The elevators were alive with laughing, babbling young women and old timers who groaned and rubbed the back of their necks.

One day, with no assignment, I opened a book, probably "Crime and Punishment" or "Anna Karenina". I was hot for the Russians back then. Miss S came up, leaned over my shoulder and looked at the title. I was surprised by her sudden interest in good literature.

"What are you doing?"

"Reading."

"That's not allowed."

"I don't have anything to do. You haven't given me anything."

"That doesn't matter. Take the time to practice. That way you'll improve your speed, without losing any accuracy."

Even though I was a liar and a cheat, I was ambitious. I got better. I got faster and more accurate and she began to love me. I was her pride and joy. So much so, that when a special typing job came down to the pool from a sales manager upstairs, Boss Lady smiled and ushered me into her cubicle. She said this letter had to be done right away and since I had improved so much, she would give the job to me. She trusted me. I should be happy.

The letter was a full page pep-talk from the manager to each of his salesmen. It began "It's good to be agressive but not too agressive."

Each salesman working for this manager would get the identical letter, except for his name of course. My job was to type sixty-five letters which I knew would be filed in the waste paper basket after reading the first paragraph. If I did a good job, I would be promoted to the next highest level—statistical typist. Endless columns of numbers forming wide spread sheets. The advantage? I would get to work on an electric typewriter. It was a consummation devoutly to be wished.

As Miss S handed me a box of BDAC&DC letterhead she pointed out that actually, this was an easy assignment since I didn't have to worry about carbons. For most jobs, extra copies were required.

For those too young to know, 1952 was before Xerox perfected its copier and soon became one of the best investments ever to hit Wall Street. Without a machine that produced copies, you had to create them yourself. You did it at the same time as you typed the original. You can't imagine what a tedious chore that was. Nobody in his right mind would ever dream of doing it today.

Here's how it was done.

1. You took a piece of letterhead or typing paper and placed a sheet of thin paper called "tissue" behind it, one sheet for each extra copy you needed.

2. Between each layer, you put a sheet of carbon paper, blue or black. This was such a clumsy maneuver that you usually smeared ink on your fingers.

3. You cleaned your hands and lined up the stack of top page, tissues and carbon paper to form a perfect rectangular whole.

4. You lifted the bar on the front of the typewriter, the paper bail.

5. You carefully rolled the rectangular stack into the narrow space behind the carriage roller and the platen.

6. You snapped the paper bail into place.

After all this, by striking the keys with the exact optimum force, the extra copies would be clear enough to read. Of course, if you screwed up on the top page, you either learned to erase each sheet very carefully, or you had to do it all over again. "White Out" was not allowed.

So when Boss Lady gave me the assignment, I sighed and said of course I would give it my best shot. *Well, it's only sixty-five letters and I'll get faster with each one—without losing accuracy.*

I did it, and when Miss S proofread the batch she only found a few letters that needed to be typed again. A job well done! Out for lunch and a cigarette! Smiling!

Back from lunch and I knew something was up as Boss Lady approached with another box of letterhead and a mournful expression in her duplicitous eyes.

"You have to do them again."

"All of them?"

"Yes Martha. I'm terribly sorry."

"But you proofread them. You said they were perfect!"

"I know. But Martha, you never noticed that the word aggressive has two "G"s.

I gasped. My faced grew red in fury.

"Neither did you. Neither did he. I *can't* do them again."

"You must."

I choked back the tears and whimpered, "Please! Please give them to someone else."

"No," she said with that shit-eating grin she was so good at, "You're the best we have."

By late August I was exhausted, hot and angry—ready for revenge. I had become very good and was truly valuable as I sat at the damned electric statistical typewriter with its extra wide carriage and sweated over every stinking decimal point.

One by one, the other college-bound girls had gone in and given three or four weeks' notice. By the third resignation, Miss S screamed "Get out! Now! You can stop in Personnel and pick up your final check!" The glass window trembled as she slammed the door.

Patiently, I waited until the time was right—the middle of August. I went to Boss Lady's cubicle, smiled politely and asked if she had a moment to speak to me. I told her that the Brooklyn Public Library where I used to work called me and invited me back. They offered me seven dollars more a week than I was earning at BDAC&DC. It was a very good opportunity for me. I could walk to work and save the hour and a half commute time not to mention the subway fare. With all the time I saved and the twenty-eight extra dollars a month, I would be able to go to college after all.

It wasn't quite a total lie. When I finished high school, the head librarian said I was welcome to come back as a full time employee. Full time help got twenty cents more an hour than part time help. There would always be a job for me checking out books, collecting two cents a day for each overdue book and picking up all the oversized picture books from the floor in the children's room and re-alphabetizing them on the shelf every night.

I got to stay in the typing pool until the end of August. I received a hearty handshake and a pat on the back for a job well done!

Between Jobs

It was September 1952. I walked into Brooklyn College to attend my first course, Basic Speech—just in case we hadn't learned to speak before.

Somehow, I had survived the hazing all incoming freshmen were required to endure. The smart students, those admitted without taking the College Boards, had to take a test anyway, a grueling 5-hour entrance exam used for "placement purposes". Somehow, I was never "placed". I was just stuck.

Once we passed the written test, we had to pass a physical to make sure we were healthy enough to be admitted. I thought they were trying to find anyone who might need special facilities like elevators or ramps. It turned out that wasn't it at all.

There were long lines in the gym. Women were sent to the right, men to the left. My group was herded into a large dressing room without partitions or curtains. We were greeted by an attractive, sweet young nurse who smiled as she said "Please take off all your clothes and hang them on a hook. All includes bras and panties, socks or stockings and shoes. Thanks so much."

She gave each of us a thin grey robe and told us to put it on, front to back. The last time I took off all my clothes in public I was probably four. The gown wouldn't close so it seemed I had my rear end framed.

We were weighed and measured and given a cup to pee in. I went to the common bathroom and did the best I could. The nurse snickered when she saw my pathetic offering.

I went for a chest X-ray. The small nurse was replaced by a tall, strong-armed nurse.

"Drop the gown!"

She pushed me against a cold glass plate, put her mouth by my ear and whispered "Breathe! Hold it!" So I did.

I took my paperwork and waited on a bench until the doctor would see me. My body was one solid goose bump and some of my parts were frozen. *This must be the final test. What else could there possibly be? An EKG? Are they afraid my heart can't stand the strain? Or maybe an EEG to see if my brain has enough empty space left for all the knowledge they intend to squeeze in?*

Finally, I was beckoned into the inner sanctum where a tired elderly doctor was waiting with his stethoscope hanging limply from his neck.

The nurse drew the curtain closed around us. Again, I was ordered to take off my gown and drop it. Then I was poked and prodded and thumped. The doctor wrote some notes on my chart while the nurse shook her head.

"Your weight is far too high. You are way over the guide-lines set by our insurance company. You go on a diet and lose at least twenty pounds by the end of the semester or you will be asked to leave."

Impossible! Summa Cum Laude and I could be expelled for twenty pounds of excess fat?

The final test came on registration day. Freshman had to choose between required courses: English Composition, European History, Basic Economics and a slew of other subjects all of which would prepare us for the real world.

There was no choice when it came to physical training. Gym was a must. It was a well-known fact that women hated gym. To make it more palatable, we were allowed to choose which activity we preferred. I took fencing. It didn't seem nearly as bad as gymnastics or soccer. Actually I enjoyed fencing. In my dreadful gym suit, protective padding and a mask to hide my face, I looked fearsome. All I had to do was advance quickly, waving my supple epée. My opponent would take one look, drop her sword and run. I got an A+ in gym.

Freshmen registered last and we were admitted to the gym to register in alphabetic order. Mintz was pretty far back on the list so I rushed from table to table trying to register for courses with the best professors. I already heard who the best were and who I should definitely avoid. By that time most of the good guys were booked. "Sorry. Try another professor."

How could I complain? The whole country was in trouble too. WWII was over and the misery was quietly tucked away. The troops came home and the veterans received the G.I. Bill to help finance their education and get low-interest mortgages.

They found their old sweethearts, got married and produced a vast number of baby boomers.

The returning men were strangely silent. They didn't talk about shelling or shooting or strafing. They tried to forget their friends' bodies that were never to be found. They couldn't speak of the horrors of Auschwitz and Bergen-Belsen. And so, their wives would never understand the screams in the middle of the night. The war was over. It was put to rest.

Peace was a mirage. By 1952 we were fighting a new war in Korea. North Korea was communist territory; South Korea was part of the "free world". The north invaded the south and the free world retaliated. The cold war melted as the Korean War grew hot.

I had a sense of betrayal when I heard the news on the radio. I was only seventeen and I had witnessed one disaster after another. I was there for the Great Depression, WWII, the Holocaust and now, this latest obscenity on the Korean peninsula. I realized that what my teachers said was true after all. We refuse to learn from our past mistakes. We think history is irrelevant. The times have changed and we think we're free to do it differently. But we have simply made our own new mistakes and have created our own new disasters.

President Truman's approval rating was at an all-time low and the economy was in the pits. The outlook was grim. Men couldn't find work. Women could be teachers, nurses, receptionists or "Gal Fridays". Some women became bookkeepers. Smart women became "Executive Secretaries". They did whatever an executive asked them to do, and they were expected to do it cheerfully. Everything from typing to stenography, from answering the phone to fetching coffee, and on to other nefarious deeds.

Billy Wilder, a brilliant movie writer and director, released a movie called "The Apartment" starring Shirley MacLaine, Jack Lemmon and the villainous Fred MacMurray. MacMurray was the selfish, sleazy manager. MacLaine was his adoring, vulnerable secretary. Jack Lemmon was his underling coerced into lending MacMurray the key to his apartment. A lot of people thought it was a comedy but it was true—it was dead-on serious.

When I graduated high school, women were still called girls. Regular girls became housewives and mothers; they were groomed for the role and did their best to do it well. But after a lifetime career of raising children and making a comfortable home for the family, a woman's work was not considered work at all. If a man was killed, the courts awarded the widow the equivalent of his future earnings. If a woman was killed, the courts awarded the widower enough money to hire a woman to keep house until the children grew up.

Suddenly, as if by providence, from out of nowhere, a whole new industry appeared. It was work for engineers and egg-heads and, since there was no precedent to follow, women could apply. The field was a mystery. But if a woman was somewhat brave and could accept the disdain of the men around her, if she was very lucky and perhaps a bit pushy, a woman just *might* find a real career.

In 1952 program was not a verb, programmer was not a noun, and programming was not a profession.

It was the summer of 1952 and both the Democrats and Republicans were courting General Dwight D. Eisenhower to be their presidential candidate. He was the great general who had masterminded our victory in Europe and had become the Supreme Commander of all NATO forces. A perfect candidate for either party. Years later, he was the sage who warned us to "beware of the military-industrial complex". But as we all know, Americans don't take advice too often and we don't accept criticism very well.

Ike ran on the Republican ticket and won. He would have won no matter where his name was on the ballot.

Go back in time to 1938 for a moment. A brilliant cryptanalyst named Alan Turing invented a machine used to break "Enigma", the highly sophisticated German code used during WWII. His machine was the ancestor of all computers to come.

In the '40s, two talented engineers, John Mauchly and J. Presper Eckert followed in Turing's footsteps and invented a new machine they called the "ENIAC" (Electronic Numerical Integrator And Computer). It could perform computations at break-neck speeds measured in milliseconds (1,000 steps a second) and microseconds (1,000,000 steps a second).

The ENIAC became the BINAC (BINary Automatic Computer) which morphed into the UNIVAC (UNIVersal Automatic Computer). The UNIVAC I was the first commercially sold computer in the world.

By 1952, the engineering duo were working in the Eckert-Mauchley Division of Sperry Rand. Remington Rand was also a division of Sperry Rand, and was best known for its typewriters and rifles. The machine was known as Remington Rand's UNIVAC. Actually the Eckert-Mauchley division was responsible for creating the equipment. Remington was responsible for sales and programming support.

Remington didn't know very much about electronic equipment. They knew very little about how to build a UNIVAC and even less about what it could do. And they didn't have a clue how to sell it, as witnessed by the fact that IBM swept the market away within just a few years. People would come to the UNIVAC display room and ask to see the latest IBM computer.

In short, no one knew what programmers were or what they were worth.

When I was hired as a programmer trainee in 1956, the job was regarded as some sort of high level clerical position with a starting salary of $4,000 a year.

UNIVAC was no surprise to the engineering world. But to the general public it was one of the best kept secrets in history, on a par with the Manhattan Project at Los Alamos. Remington wanted something special to demonstrate to the whole world what their electronic phenomenon could do. It had to be something memorable. The Madison Avenue hucksters came up with a "brainy" idea, sales-wise that is.

Every four years, on the first Tuesday in November, Americans stayed up well into the night to find out who their next President would be. There were polling places all across the country. In cities, voting booths were set up in schools and churches and wherever public space was available. Long lines of people waited for hours to cast their ballots. In the rural areas people would travel miles to exercise their right to vote.

There were paper ballots and pencils in curtained booths so each citizen was ensured the right to a secret ballot. For some, voting was the fulfillment of a dream. For women, it was a cherished right they won in 1920. Negroes got the right to vote in 1870, fifty years earlier, but they were still fighting that battle. Poll taxes and literacy tests in most of the Deep South were used to keep them away. Public sentiment everywhere kept women away.

Collecting all this paper and counting all the pencil marks was a slow, laborious procedure. As each polling place closed, final counts were made, and results were ticker-taped to election headquarters. We would stay awake for hours listening to the radio, excited as new numbers were announced. Some of us fancied ourselves students of higher mathematics, wrote the statistics down and tried to make predictions ourselves. Sometimes, the outcome of an election wasn't known until Wednesday when the final returns arrived from the "Far West": California, Oregon and Washington. A lot of people stayed awake the whole time until a reasonable, trustworthy prediction was announced. Archaic? Well I remember waiting over a week before the Supreme Court decided who had won.

In 1952 a group of statisticians sat at election headquarters with sharpened pencils and large erasers. Party loyal servants stood in front of a giant blackboard and posted the counts for everyone to see. Excitement rose as each new tally arrived. How soon would they predict the outcome? Faster than last year, we hoped. And each time a new figure was posted, the most talented men in probability theory put their heads together to arrive at a single group prediction.

Against this backdrop, the Remington pundits decided to pit the UNIVAC against the statisticians. As numbers arrived from around the country they were simultaneously posted on the board and entered into the computer. Even though we knew there was no such thing as an "electronic brain", tensions mounted. It was "Man against Machine". Which one would win the challenge of the nerds?

By 8:30 Tuesday night, based on a small sample of voters and long before the West Coast polls even closed, UNIVAC predicted it would be Eisenhower by a landslide. Opinion polls had predicted his chance of winning was 1 in 100. The Democratic candidate, Adlai Stevenson was a shoo-in. At CBS the executives decided the machine was wrong. They didn't even announce the details of the failure. Instead they declared the "electronic brain" didn't have the IQ of a first grader.

But the UNIVAC programmers stood firm. A small problem that showed up early in the evening was fixed. They stuck to their guns. As history has shown, just as the UNIVAC predicted, Ike carried the day.

By 1953 things hadn't improved much. The Cold War was still going strong and on the home front, everyone was under suspicion. Senator Joe McCarthy and his sidekick, Roy Cohn, were shouting about Communists and Commie Sympathizers infiltrating the country. He denounced anyone he wanted to. People who had once believed in liberal left-wing causes were accused. People McCarthy didn't like were attacked. The government was maligned. Movie stars were blacklisted. Scientists who had saved the country in WWII were accused of treason. McCarthy waved his infamous lists in the air. People named names of their colleagues and friends to pacify the bloodthirsty beast. Ethel and Julius Rosenberg were electrocuted.

The senator from Wisconsin was un-stoppable. It was a long time before people saw him for what he was worth, a bully and an obnoxious, sleazy politician. Everyone hated McCarthy's tricks. Everyone that is, except J. Edgar Hoover who loved it all.

It was 1953 and I needed another job.

One Step Closer

June 1953. I sat opposite a placement expert at an employment agency that specialized in clerical work. She smiled wearily when I told her I wanted a summer job in an office, but my office skills were limited. *Not another one,* she thought.

"Well, what *can* you do?"

"I can type 50 words a minute. And I can file."

"Can you answer the phone and take messages?"

"Yes."

"Can you take shorthand?"

"No."

She spun her Rolodex, shuffled through some index cards, and frowned. Eventually she found a job for Thursday and Friday to replace a girl on sick leave. Maybe she could find something better by the end of the week. The take home pay was $11 a day (1/5 of the standard $55 a week), so it would come to $22 less the 15% agency fee. The job was on 4th Avenue in Manhattan, an hour each way on the subway from Brooklyn. It wasn't much for a girl who had just finished her first year of college with a modest B+ average. But it was a real temporary job and I was not prepared to lie about my college plans like I did the summer before.

I took the job in a quiet, hot office working for a quiet, cool lady. I called her Mrs. Something and she called me Martha thereby establishing my position in the hierarchy. The days were not grey here, but sort of a colorless beige. This placement was a laugh. I should have waited for something more substantial. I'd be out of work by Saturday. But, I worked all day Thursday and Friday and at the end, I went to my boss to get my time sheet approved. After the agency fee I was left with $18.70 less withholding and Social Security. She signed the time sheet, asked me to take a seat and dialed the Personnel Department.

"I have a bright college girl here. She knows how to type, she can spell, she takes messages correctly and she's very polite and quiet."

Listening.

"If you have any other openings for summer temps, I think you ought to hire her." Pause.

"Good. You call the agency and I'll tell Martha where to report on Monday." Turning to me she asked, "Is that OK with you?"

"Yes. Thank you *so* much."

"Go to the 10th floor on Monday morning. The UNIVAC people are up there. I don't exactly *know* what they do. They need someone to type an instruction manual. It's a six or seven week assignment. Is that OK with you?"

You bet it was! That would keep me employed until school started in the fall. I could worry about money after that.

"Be sure to introduce yourself and see Ruth, the Administrative Assistant. She's another one up there but I don't know what she does either."

I murmured my thanks.

"You have a good future, my dear," she said, "You are very bright and a college girl can go far here at Remington Rand. You have excellent secretarial skills."

At 8:30 on Monday morning I came up out of the 23rd Street station on the BMT line and took a good look around at my summer home. I walked along the south side of Madison Park from 5th Avenue to 4th. I looked up at number 315, a big square brick building with nothing much to recommend it. The heat was oppressive. The subway felt like an oven and, in 1953, most offices were not air-conditioned. Just like last year, this job would be a modern version of a Roman bath. Only the 2nd floor was air-conditioned. That was the home of the one-of-a-kind UNIVAC electronic brain which survived only in cool dry air. Employees, on the other hand, survived everywhere—easy to replace.

I walked in and saw eleven elevators—cage-like affairs you see in movies set in post-war Europe. The thrillers where people are murdered by being pushed into empty elevator shafts? When you were in an elevator you would note the empty spaces where adjoining elevators travelled up and down. The cables looked thick *enough* until you realized how many *bodies* were squeezed into those boxes with you.

I had to feel sorry for the exhausted, pathetic elevator operators who sported stiff tan shirts and brown pants with shiny stripes down the side of each leg. To top it off, they wore matching brown jackets and bow-ties. Each man's job was to maneuver a lever that made the elevator rise or fall. That lever was the only thing that stood between life and death.

Kind elevator men guided passengers smoothly from floor to floor and gently came to rest. The ones who had had a fight with their wives that morning, whooshed through the dark chutes and stopped so abruptly your heart rushed from your chest to your stomach and back again. These sadists left some space between the open door level and the floor so you might flop into the office like a beached whale. Clerks and lower management walked to the back and took the local rides. Upper management and corporate bigwigs took the express elevators at the front reserved just for them.

Elevators stopped at the requested floors. When you got into the elevator you called out your floor loud and clear. If you didn't, you had to wait while the cage continued to the end of the line—the 17th floor. There the operator stepped out to stretch his legs and get a breath of fresh air, returned to his post and set you down in the place where you belong.

His was a hot and boring job and the pay was pitiful. Endless hours of up and down, up and down like a yo-yo could make a person bi-polar. Nonetheless, a few of the operators were cheerful and had a penchant for flirting with the prettiest passengers. The highest compliment a girl could receive was a hopeful operator asking for her phone number. Of course it was futile. There was a strict class system at work here and the elevator men were stuck in the basement.

The Remington building faced the Met Life building on the opposite side of the street. It was beautiful. Its tower rose majestically and its bells signaled the passage of time with deep resonant chimes that marked the beginning and end of our work day.

On 23rd Street near the Met Life building there was Madison Park, a small park with benches where I would sit, Monday thru Thursday, eating a bag lunch I brought from home. On Fridays, I perched on a stool at Chock Full O' Nuts savoring their famous date & nut bread with cream cheese sandwiches and a cup of steaming coffee.

On the first day of work, when I stepped out onto the 10th floor I nearly dropped my sandwich. Young men and women were laughing and drinking coffee and having a terrific time. Whatever they were doing, it wasn't secretarial and I was determined that I would do it too.

Ruth ushered me to my own private desk equipped with a shiny new Remington manual typewriter. "Don't expect too much or you'll only be disappointed," my mother's voice echoed in my head. "What did you expect, an electric typewriter? Consider yourself lucky to have a job at all!"

There was an endless supply of coffee, doughnuts, schnecken and bagels with cream cheese. We got the leftovers after impressive presentations hosted for industry moguls—potential UNIVAC buyers. They were about to spend millions of dollars, so they got goodies in the morning and fancy alcoholic lunches at noon.

Ruth gave me a full box of typing paper, and a handwritten manuscript entitled "Basic UNIVAC Programming."

I learned a lot that summer.

I learned that UNIVAC was the amazing machine unveiled on Election Day and these happy people were the ones that made it work. They had confounded the pundits. I was privileged to work with them.

I learned that this weird assemblage had been hired straight out of college. Most of them didn't have any idea what they would be doing, but they took up the challenge, gave it a shot, and were off on a whirlwind of excitement and satisfaction. A few of them were math or engineering students but some were English majors, some had studied Art History, some had majored in languages and spoke fluent French and Spanish and Italian, with a smattering of broken German. It really didn't matter.

As I typed the manual, I learned that a computer was nothing more than an over-sized calculator that could do arithmetic, but had the ability to compare different numbers and do different things depending on something I couldn't quite fathom. It was a huge contraption, 1,250 square feet, consisting of a complicated array of mercury acoustic delay lines, vacuum tubes and cables as far as the eye could see. It filled a whole room and was big enough to walk into. Every Wednesday, the UNIVAC was unavailable as the engineers took the system "down" for preventive maintenance. The concept of preventing failures on a timed, regular basis went out with the arrival of the Personal Computer. Out of the Windows, so to speak. We could peer into the axons and synapses of this old brain. Sometimes, one of the engineers would even let us walk in to look—but not touch.

I learned there was a special procedure called a program that showed the computer what steps to follow in order to produce the correct results for any given problem. The people who created these procedures were the real brains behind the brain and were called programmers.

I also learned that there was a reward for paying attention, finding mistakes and reporting them. I was gaily typing away, learning the difference between milliseconds and microseconds, when I came across a sentence that read, "So naturally, if x=20, then 2x=200".

"I think you have a mistake in your manual."

Gene glanced up with that doubtful look I knew so very well.

"Oh? Really?"

"This equation is wrong."

Disbelief.

"A typist who reads? Who understands algebra? My God, you shouldn't be a clerk! You should be a programmer!" Taking it to an extreme he added, "Now listen, anything else you see that doesn't make any sense, you come straight to me. Even if you're not sure."

Before I left at the end of August they invited me back. They could always use a bright college girl they said. "And, when you graduate, you can be a programmer right here. Just let us know, and we'll get you into the next training class." I suggested that when I came back as a clerk next summer, they should hire me directly. The company would save the agency fee and we could split the difference for my pay. Being in the real world for only a few months, I had learned how it worked.

Before the fall semester began, I went back to Remington and spoke to Gene and told him I really didn't want to finish college. I would be much happier to start training right away. He said that would be a big mistake. A college education was a valuable thing. Besides, the only requirement for the job was a college diploma. I asked what I should study, what major he recommended.

"Anything you want, it really doesn't matter. We do all the training right here in this department. So study what you like. It might help to take some math but Symbolic Logic would be the most useful thing you can learn."

The Invitation

September 1952. Brooklyn College. A new way of learning. Boys became men. Girls became ladies. Names came with titles: Mr., Miss and an occasional Mrs.

There were four free colleges in New York City. Brooklyn and Queens Colleges were in the "outer boroughs". Manhattan was home to Hunter College and the city's flagship school, City College. All of them were free to any NYC high school graduate who lived in any one of New York's five boroughs. I should say, they were virtually free. Tuition was $6 per semester. Lab fees were $15 per lab. Books were not covered. But books were simple in the '50s. No eye-catching covers, no glossy pages, no illustrations. Just no-nonsense instructive books without any answers in the back.

College Board exams were the SATs of the day and admission was based on both high school average and College Board results. At BC, girls were admitted automatically if they graduated with at least a 90% average. No questions asked. Boys needed 85%. Everyone knew that girls applied themselves to their education. Their homework was completed on time, test scores were high and their behavior was impeccable. Boys were more laid back. They were happy playing ball and fooling around after school. A few demerits and an occasional detention didn't faze them one bit. They were noisy and boisterous. They had no manners. Boys would get into fights and hit each other. Girls, on the other hand, specialized in ridicule and ostracism.

There was one thing that boys did much, much better than girls. Physical things. Boys took "Phys Ed" and wore tee-shirts and shorts. They did push-ups and climbed ropes and somersaulted over padded stuffed horses. Girls took "gym" and wore one piece gym suits with bloomers. We did deep knee bends, learned folk dancing and for a break, played a polite game of volleyball.

Boys walked around in scruffy sneakers and showed off their budding muscles. Girls walked around with books clutched tightly in front of their chests. Some tried to hide their flat chests, and the others knew that breasts could get you in trouble.

But it wasn't grades or behavior that accounted for gender discrimination. The bar was set higher for girls so that the ratio of males to females would be better. If the 90% average rule applied to everybody, there wouldn't be too many males in the new incoming classes. The practice was not only unfair, it was disgraceful.

In order to understand Brooklyn College you must understand disappointment. Fading dreams, lost hopes, bleak days. At BC, disappointment was the order of the day.

For me, disappointment was an albatross dangling from my neck—a block of cement on my feet. Why was I here?

Why not Cornell or Radcliffe or even Vassar for God's sake? My glorious past meant nothing. I was just one body in the mob of over 1,000 incoming freshmen. Total enrollment was about 10,000 students, including those getting Master Degrees. There were no doctoral level courses. It stood to reason that New York City wouldn't pay for a PhD.

In September, teachers who taught basic composition, speech, college algebra, introductory geology—all returned to their posts with disappointment in their hearts. They deserved better than this.

Even the maintenance people who kept the buildings clean and tended the lawns and shoveled the snow were disappointed. Theirs was a dead end job.

In October, I was summoned to meet Dean McNamara, the energetic, round-faced Dean of Girls who shook my hand and introduced me to my Guidance Counselor. Miss Stevenson was sluggish, square jawed and bored to death. She was disappointed ever since the post of Assistant Dean of Girls went to a younger, inexperienced but absolutely enthusiastic twit.

Miss Stevenson was supposed to help me adjust to Academia and guide me in my choice of major. She would prepare me for the Real World.

"Well Martha. What are you interested in?"

"Math and science. I want that for my major. For a minor I was thinking of world lit or psychology. I like the combination. Something to sharpen my mind and something you can talk about at parties."

"You can't take math or science."

"Why not?"

"Math and science are not for girls. They're too hard."

"But I was an A student at Midwood. I was in Agathon and Arista and I loved math and I got 98 on the Regent exams and took as much science as I could. I even won the Biology medal when I graduated!"

"You still don't understand. It's not your ability that counts."

"What don't I understand? What's that about ability?"

"If you take physics, you have to spend long hours in the lab twice a week. It's too tiring. In the winter you wouldn't get out of lab until after dark—and you'll be surrounded by young men."

"That's ridiculous. What's wrong with the hours and the dark and the young men?"

"You'd be a fish out of water."

This was no simile; it was a metaphor and as such had to be obeyed. I had to take all the required courses first—the introductory ones—Philosophy 1.1, English 1.1—Speech 1.1. If you did well in 1.1 you could skip directly to 2.1. Under achievers had to take 1.2 and total wash-outs had to try 1.1 again. It was a system made up of ones, twos and decimal points. If you continued to fail a required course, you could be thrown out of school altogether.

I left the Dean's Office—disappointed. I had to find another major.

My French had always been top-notch. I could study and become a French teacher with a meteoric rise to Professor of French Drama and Comedy. Students of Molière and Racine would murmur my name—praise my wisdom. My first advanced French course consisted of students from France or Quebec. I had better change my major.

So I thought I would be an English major teaching creative writing at the Iowa State after having published my first novel that was short-listed for the National Book Award. But my English composition professor told me I suffered from "diarrhea of the mouth".

What to do? Education majors were a boring lot but they at least had a future ahead of them. I was an academic student, so bookkeeping and stenography were out of the question. The only other respectable job for women was nursing. That was a different college.

Every semester my father would ask if I had registered for any Ed courses. I didn't want to teach at any level of the public school system and he knew it. He thought I should take Ed as a minor so that I would have something "to fall back on" even though he and I didn't have the slightest idea what I would fall back from. My frivolous attitude would lead to a bleak future, he said. I had to have something to do in case I never got married.

After my summer at Remington Rand, I felt liberated. I had a goal. I would be a programmer, whatever that was, and would work with the UNIVAC. So I learned what I needed to get a degree. I took a bunch of 1.1 and 2.1 courses and even had some 3.0 and 4.0 classes now and then.

Despite Miss Stevenson's advice I took Analytic Geometry planning to be a math major. There were two women in a class of twenty-eight students. Math was looking better every minute.

Like everyone else, Mrs. Levy, our instructor, was a disappointed soul. She was up for promotion but lost out to a man with obviously inferior talent. She had to vent on somebody; her students were sitting ducks.

"How many of you have chosen math as your major?"

What a stupid question! Who in his right mind would take this course if he weren't a math major?

Twenty-six hands shot up.

"Well," she said, "we'll see about that."

Mrs. Levy taught by example—no explanations. Each sample problem was written on the board and a series of equations followed. We had to take the answer on faith. Only the best and the brightest could figure out how she did it. I ruled out math.

I decided to be a psychology major instead. I hated the psychology 1.1 professor so I dropped down an academic notch and became a sociology major. Sociology was a woman's major—freewheeling—not too demanding. We learned a little bit about a lot of things and ended up dilettantes. The only benefit women derived from this course of study was the ability to sound clever at dinner parties after washing diapers all day.

It wasn't until my senior year that I discovered that what I liked best were the men's courses, "Statistics for the Social Sciences" and "Symbolic Logic". I aced them both. There was hope for me yet.

The next two summers I returned as a clerk typist to my UNIVAC job. It had become my safety net, my home away from home. Each August I would be invited back again. Everybody said, "When you're ready to work as a programmer, come back and the job is yours." Only one thing was a bit troubling to me. Programmers were intelligent happy people, enthused and delighted about a machine. What about culture—art—literature—Matisse? Would I fit in?

There were a few women working at UNIVAC. Not many mind you, but for women, more than two was a triumph. There was a likely explanation for this. It was a new field. No one knew much about it. I don't think anyone ever anticipated that this was the way for the weaker sex to have a career in a first class profession. It was unheard of and that made it a little suspect as well. It couldn't be anything to brag about if women were included.

During all this time I was dating Bob Wilensky, my high school boyfriend. He was a "Bohemian" who wore a beret and ascot and took me to concerts and museums and gave me high-brow books to read.

On dates we went to some cultural event, saw every movie that came out, or walked down Ocean Avenue singing folk songs in harmony all the way. We went to Lundy's Oyster Bar and ordered clam chowder and ate all the biscuits they put on the table. Then we said we were too full to order anything else so just bring the check please.

Sometimes we took the subway to Coney Island where Bob would hit long drives at "Bat-a-Way" while I tried my hand at shooting metal ducks on moving tracks. Then a walk down the boardwalk to Nathan's for a hot dog and the World's Greatest French Fries.

I was a cheap date. And a cheap drunk. We went to the Studio Bar on Avenue M right next door to the NBC Studio. Bob ordered a few beers and I nursed a small red wine. We sat there all night talking about James Joyce and Dylan Thomas and Emanuel Kant. Sometimes a TV star would wander in for a drink.

My parents hated Bob and everyone thought I was a little crazy. Undaunted, we were waiting until we both graduated Brooklyn College to tie the knot.

By the end of my sophomore year I settled on sociology as my major with a minor in psychology. I was half way towards my diploma and had to pick something. I studied hard and daydreamed about the day when I would finish and put all this behind me.

After graduation, I had to choose between two possible jobs. I could be a Social Investigator for the NYC Department of Welfare. That meant I would go into dismal areas of the city and try to catch anyone who was cheating and collecting $25 a week from the government. It meant surprising a single mother living on welfare who was already getting $10 a week from a sympathetic old-maid aunt. Or tracking down a married woman who claimed she had been abandoned leaving her with no money to feed the kids when actually she had a faithful husband who simply couldn't make ends meet.

I was expected to root out cheating old ladies who didn't need any help because they lived with their children or grandchildren anyway. It meant becoming a spy—a fink—an agent of a heartless society that wanted the problem to just go away.

Or, I could become a programmer on 4th Avenue trying to learn some unfathomable skill that still was a mystery to me.

Social Investigators earned $4,200 a year. Programmers only got $4,000. How to make such a decision? I didn't have to. It was soon decided for me.

I knew all the sociology professors personally since my sister Barbara, was the department secretary. It was the fall and I was due to graduate right after New Year's. I got a call from the Chairman of the Sociology Anthropology Department, Prof. Alfred McClung Lee, an imposing handsome gentleman who had never done more than nod at me in the past.

Professor Lee offered me a wonderful opportunity. He would arrange for me to become the Department Fellow as soon as I completed my last course. It was a great honor, he told me. It was not usually offered in mid-year but I was special. My duties would be helping professors prepare lectures, grade papers, and participate in any research projects going on. It was very prestigious and, by the way, since Barbara was leaving, I could do the secretarial work as well.

Dumbfounded, I said I needed time to think about it, left the office and wandered the halls. Why had I even bothered to come? What good was my education anyway? What was he thinking? How come he didn't offer the job to J. J. Morris who was certainly the best sociology major they had?

The hell with them! I would have a college degree and I could do better! The next day I politely declined the offer. I was going to become a computer programmer.

The whole department was aghast. Didn't I realize that being a Fellow was a prestigious position? They were counting on me to say "yes". Only one professor thought about me. He told me to go out and learn all I could and come back to him and he would show me how to merge technology and the social sciences. Thank heavens for Professor Erickson!

I graduated in January and never went back to pick up my diploma at the formal graduation ceremony in June.

Finally, December 1955 came along. I appeared at the UNIVAC office and announced that I was ready to start work in January. There was a Basic Programming course beginning on the 15th. Could I be ready by that time? I could and I would. There was no aptitude test, no college grades to be examined, no references required. My future was sealed. I would be a computer programmer!

I looked around and thought:
> ". . . *oh brave new world*
> *That has such people in't!*"